Sword of a Messenger

Wind of Destiny, Volume Eight

AJ Cooper

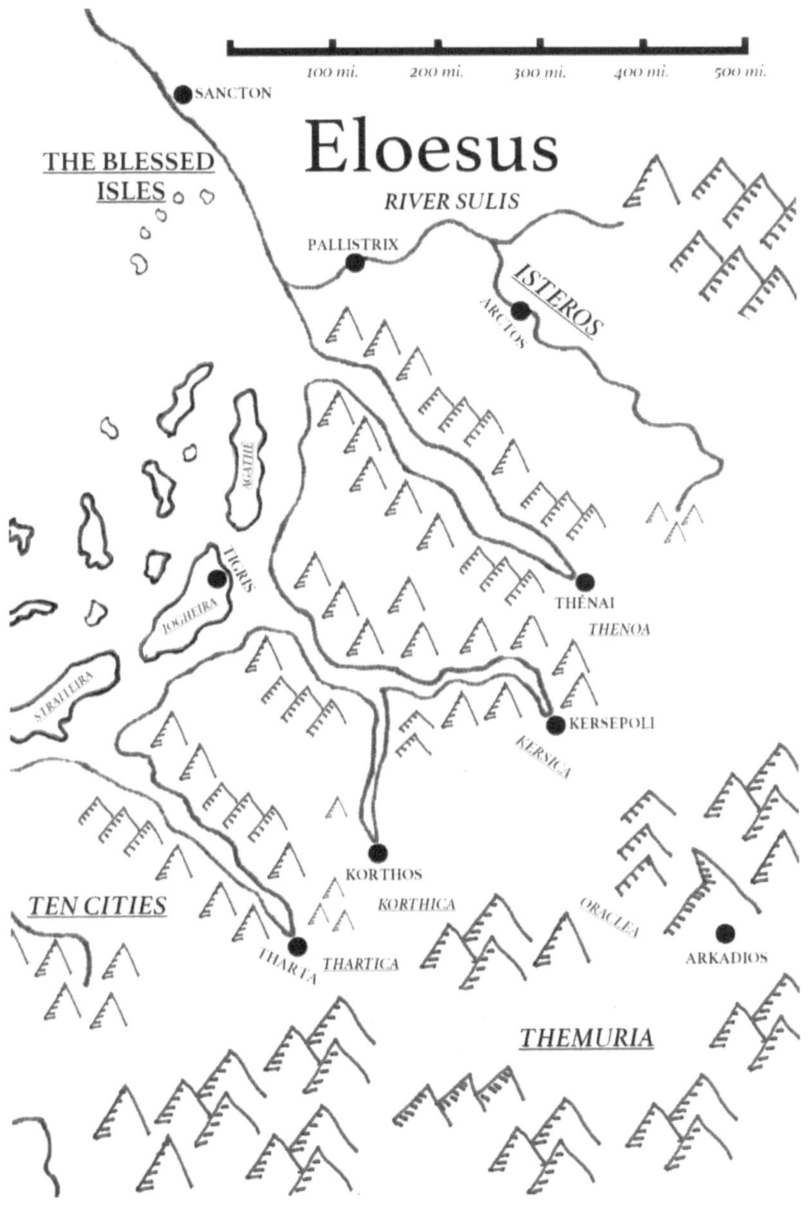

SANCTON
THE BLESSED ISLES
Eloesus
RIVER SULIS
PALLISTRIX
ISTEROS
ARCTOS
AGATHE
TIGRIS
IOGHEIRA
STRATTEIRA
THÉNAI
THENOA
KERSEPOLI
KERSICA
KORTHOS
KORTHICA
ORACLEA
TEN CITIES
ARKADIOS
THARTA
THARTICA
THEMURIA
100 mi.
200 mi.
300 mi.
400 mi.
500 mi.

THE DEPARTURE

Outside the gate of Kersepoli, children had gathered to play. The sun beat down hot, scorching the flat plains surrounding the city, and the streams which interwove the landscape in the springtime had all dried up. Cows and sheep panted in the heat, tormented by flies as they sweltered in silence. Perhaps, the children thought, the summer would never end; winter would never come, bringing its refreshing cool and its driving rain. Perhaps, the sun would swallow them all up, and the earth, as they knew it, would perish in fire.

Out of the gate strode a man in a headband, brown of hair, and the children looked up from their games to gawk. In his right hand he had a sling, and in his left a sword. At his belt, a sack full of stones was tied. He left with seeming determination and focus, though what his determination and focus was, the children could only guess.

Soon, the man in the headband was gone, and the children continued their games, throwing ball or hiding in the grass. It was far too hot to run.

The sun and summer would swallow them all up, but the man in the headband had left the city briskly, with a purpose in his heart.

HELĒMON AND THE NORTH WIND

A FABLE

One day, the hero Helēmon was wandering the land of Dys, and found himself standing at the pillars which mark the western edge of the world. Beyond the sea, the North Wind was blowing, tossing up the waves in a violent storm. The North Wind saw the valuable cloak Helēmon was wearing and vowed to take it from him.

The North Wind blew with all his might, attempting to throw the cloak of Helēmon off his back. But the more the North Wind blew, the tighter Helēmon wrapped his cloak. At last, the North Wind ceased its tumultuous gusts and the sky cleared, giving way to the bright sun, a gentle warmth, and a cool breeze. By the shores of the sea, Helēmon lay down and removed his cloak. Sometimes, force is not necessary to get what you want.

—Amalchio

HILL COUNTRY, THENOA

For days, Geon had wandered away from Thénai. He did not know where he was going. Bright white wings had emerged on his back, allowing the wind to course by him quickly, but try as he might, he couldn't fly. Whenever a shepherd saw him in the hills, they fled in terror. He would never again be accepted by his fellow humans; of that, he was sure. And as for saving the city of Thénai, there was no purpose. The city had, against all odds, been reclaimed. The flags of the Thenoan League now flapped over its turrets and battlements. What purpose, then, was there for drinking the Stygian water? He had gained power anew, and a vast endurance, but now he was scorned and feared wherever he went. He was marked for different. Theron, the hero of the Southron War, had been given great strength and prowess, but he had not been turned into a monster. Geon had; and for what reason? There was none.

He would return the Spear and Shield of Pegara to their place; he would lay them to rest in the cold waters of the grotto far north of Thénai. Then, the sickness would consume Geon, and he would die.

~

Over weeks and days, up and down the rolling hills and in and out of the meandering roads, Geon — bearing Pegara's Spear and Shield — traveled throughout the region of Thenoa. At last, mountains appeared, covered in pines and cypress trees. The road continued, winding its way up the impossibly high peak. He was on the border of the Kingdom of Isteros, which Thénai viewed with absolute disdain. Thenoans thought the Isteroi were barbarians, but who was and who was not a barbarian no longer concerned Geon. The war between the Kersican and Thenoan Leagues no longer concerned Geon. It all seemed so petty, these battles and conflicts, this strife between brothers. None of it mattered. Nothing did.

The road wound its way up the mountains, beside waterfalls and babbling brooks, and near icy ponds where Geon stopped to drink. "Pegara," he whispered to a hero long dead and long forgotten, whose spear and shield he was carrying, "I will return your weapons to you soon."

The spear and shield were not Geon's; they belonged to another. They belonged in the sacred grotto, here, in these mountains… here, on the roof of the world.

~

When he reached the grotto, he was not alone. A young woman was there, in a white dress and a blue-rimmed hood. The grotto was surrounded by laurel trees, and a fog had moved in. Despite the fog, oil lamps were burning, and light was plentiful. When Geon had come here for the first time, ill and in need of healing, the grotto had been abandoned. Now, the shrine was active once more, and here standing before Geon was a Maid of Prophecy, a servant of the Oracle. This grotto, a memorial of the forgotten hero Pegara, was a holy site once more. The altar, just before the water's edge, was worn away with time, but it had been renewed in function and purpose.

"Geon," the Maid said.

"You know my name," he muttered. How did she know his name? True, he had come here with other Maids of Prophecy, but this Maid he did not recognize. He had never seen her before.

"We thought you would be back," the Maid said.

"We?" he asked, though he knew just what she meant. She, and all other maids, served the Oracle. Geon had retrieved his weapons from the grotto's waters. He had even journeyed to the

Oracle's sacred mountain, but he had refused to do her bidding. Now, having disrespected her, he had become the Oracle's enemy. Looking at this young woman in her Maid's garb, he wondered if he should be afraid. Was there murder in her eyes?

"Why have you come here?" the Maid said, though Geon guessed she already knew.

"I've come to return the spear and shield. They don't belong to me. And I don't have a purpose." Geon's words were dourer than he intended. But he didn't want this life. He didn't want to be a hero. He would let the power, coursing inside him, consume him.

"The Spear and Shield of Pegara are gifts," the Maid said. "It is rude to return a gift."

"Look at me!" Geon said. With his white swan-like wings, his halo of starlight, and bright blue eyes, he had become a creature of supernal beauty, but others didn't see it that way; they reacted in terror or revulsion. This new body, this newfound power, had set him apart from his fellow Eloesians in the most unequivocal of ways. He was not a human anymore. He was something entirely different. And he could never go back to what he was.

He cast the spear and shield on the ground.

"You know," Geon said, "your master wants me dead."

The Oracle's threats were still on his mind; she had tried to kill him herself, but Geon had overpowered even her, even the greatest of beings in Eloesus.

"Let me tell you a story," the Maid said, "if you will listen."

Geon sat down by the grotto's mouth and dipped his hands into the ice-cold, inky black water.

The Maid took a seat on a high rock. "Pegara was like you, you know," she said.

"In what way?"

"She drank the Stygian water like you did… but it was by the Oracle's devising, in her case. As her power grew, she—like you—was clothed in light. She became exceedingly strong. In the Amazon-Eloesian War, which she was raised up for, she won many battles and slew many enemies. But as the years progressed, her fellow humans began to turn on her. And by the time the war was won, she was shunned altogether. She was driven out of the cities, and even the country folk wanted nothing to do with her. She was marked as different, like you are, young Geon.

"But it was turning on the Oracle, who raised her up as a hero, that was her greatest mistake. She became convinced of her great evil, and intended to slay her. But she was no match.

"In the end, it was her own people that protected the Oracle from Pegara. One night, they set upon Pegara… they cut her down with daggers and knives as she slept. Only after she was dead did they remember her warmly."

"But she was forgotten," Geon corrected her.

"She was forgotten," the Maid agreed, "but her spear and shield remained. Her power is still in them. Few remember her. Heroes have gone before her, countless heroes… Phillipidēs… Helēmon. But her grotto has remained safe."

"You know," Geon said, "I walked all the way back to Thénai… hoping to save my friends and my family. But when I got there, it was all pointless. Thénai was safe. They had recaptured the city! I drank the water only for its power. And now all this strength, all this speed… what good is it? I ruined my life for Thénai's sake. What foolishness!"

"Thénai is *not* safe," the Maid said. "In fact, its position is more perilous than ever. For reasons within and without. If your heart's desire is to save Thénai, I wish you well. But the city is doomed."

"How is it doomed?" Geon said. "It drove back the Kersicans! Its streets are reclaimed!"

"But you do not know what lies within," the Maid said, "or who is without. If you want to be a hero like Pegara, there is doom aplenty for you to overcome."

COUNCIL ROOM, HOUSE OF THE ARCHON, THÉNAI

As the archon Dioscouro babbled on and on, speaking of grain shipments from Khazidea and the resettlement of refugees in their old homes, Khloë, amazon, citizen, and member of the Council of War, watched aloofly. Over the past few days, she had found it difficult to concentrate on the war effort, on the minutiae of troop pay and reports from the spies within enemy lines. She had heard rumors of sickness spreading in Potters' Street, no doubt an effect of bodies lying to rot. She knew already the toll that the flesh flies had unleashed on Thénai, and the disfigurement they caused. Many had spoken of an increase in scorpions in city buildings, with poisonous and painful stingers.

But the thing that hung heaviest over Khloë was not the war, nor disease, nor pests, but instead the statue that now lay inside Amara's temple. She had heard only descriptions of the god that was now honored inside, only vague hints of what it might look like. The fact that southrons decided to honor a different god in Amara's temple was not surprising. What surprised her, and alarmed her deeply, was the fact that Dioscouro had sealed the temple doors, forbidding anyone to speak of the matter, and moreover, refused to remove the abomination from its place. She had begun to question everything and everyone. She had begun to wonder about Dioscouro. She had begun to wonder if she had any true friends in Thénai, and if there was anyone at all, in elite circles or in the streets of the commoners, whom she could trust.

"The Kings of Kersepoli have begun to regroup," Dioscouro was saying. "We must strike while they are still dazed…"

Khloë had spent countless hours in the council room, discussing this or that, preparing for battle, listening to reports by spies and surveyors. She had never offered any advice, or given any matter any deep thought. All she could think about was the statue in Amara's temple and how the doors were sealed and shut.

In the past months, she had ventured far from Eloesus; she had gone to the village of Bastos, halfway across the sea, where those who worshiped the Old Gods gathered, offering human sacrifices to their lord. Now an Old God was being honored in Khloë's home, the city of Thénai. It had been unthinkable. It *still* was unthinkable.

When Khloë brought up the statue to Dioscouro, he had dismissed her out of hand. He had said some bumbling thing about the Kaiaphons, a rich family who helped fund Thénai's war efforts. She was certain it was all connected. And yet, what could she do?

"Tonight, our army arrives in the Bos," Dioscouro continued. "We will drive the Kersicans out of the entire fortress. And then we will press onward. No town of the Kersican league will be safe, Amara will it."

Still they used her name, she, the chief goddess of Thénai, she, the queen of battle and wisdom and war. But her temple was desecrated, and its doors were locked shut. Already, people in Thénai had begun to worry and to talk.

~

Late in the day, as the sun was setting, Khloë left the House of the Archon and its council chamber to walk out onto the High City. The temple cast the ground around it in long shadows, and its doors, barred shut, seemed larger than before. She had begun to grow restless.

Out of the red light of dusk emerged Phalco, Dioscouro's bodyguard, a man she had come to trust. He wore the blue horsehair crested helmet of Thénai on his head, and a breastplate of bronze on his chest. Even now, when there was no danger to speak of, when the judges and magistrates had gone home and the law courts were empty, he was prepared for battle. Any unexpected threat to Thénai's government would have to come through him.

On the edge of the High City, Khloe looked down on the red roofs of the city below. Many wood frames lay unadorned, and foundations were being dug as Thénai recovered from its destruction. Most of the city had burned away, but the refugees had returned. It would take a year, at best, to get back to normal, and who knew how long to fully recover from the siege. Perhaps, there would be no recovery at all. Thénai had reached a great height before its sudden fall. Who knew if they could ever reach it again?

"Khloë," Phalco said. "It is good to see you."

Khloë was dressed in a red gown, fitted for a human woman of her size. She could feel each gust of the wind. The fabric was light. Ever since she joined Thénai's ruling caste, she had dressed this way, with elegance and refinement. Human women wore much less clothing than amazons, and let much more of the skin be revealed. Khloë didn't think she would ever get used to it.

"Are you all right?" Phalco said.

In the past, Khloë had confided in Phalco about her concerns, about her worries for the temple, how its doors were fully sealed shut. Phalco had cast those concerns aside, refusing to tell her what he knew. He had been utterly dismissive. "You know what is bothering me," Khloë told him.

In City Square, she could see a battalion of hoplites performing exercises. From this distance, they were like ants. The whole of Thénai was little more than a military camp.

Phalco pressed his spear into the dust, and ground it around, as if he were killing an insect. "I am sworn to secrecy, Khloë," he said. "I wish I could tell you."

"I am a member of the Council of War!" Khloë said. "And

they will let a member of the guard know everything, but not me."

"Even I was not supposed to know," Phalco said. "But I overheard…"

Khloë turned to him, grabbing the cuff of his cape. "Why is the temple sealed? Why won't they let anyone in?"

Phalco sighed. "Come with me, Khloë. Let's find a secret place."

Behind the Temple of Amara was an aviary, but it had fallen into disuse. The feeders had not been stocked ever since the siege began, and the shrubberies had wilted and withered away. There were no birds to be found, nor people. Once, the priestesses of Amara had tended to the area, but the priesthood was gone, scattered in the wake of the siege. Many had died, and many more had been driven away in the face of rampaging violence. Here, Khloë and Phalco were alone, with only the shadows to watch over them.

"Khloë," Phalco said, "you must swear everything to secrecy. If Dioscouro finds out I told you, he'll have me stripped of my title or worse…"

What worse was there to a hoplite than expulsion from the army?

"When we laid siege to Thénai, we had gathered forty-thousand hoplites from cities all across the sea… But there was no resistance! The southrons and the Kersicans had turned on each other, and the city was desolate. But when we ascended the High City, we saw the temple doors were wide open, and in the sanctuary was a god that no one recognized. It was a monstrous thing…

"We intended to melt it down into bronze and discard it. We were all disgusted. We were just about to remove it from its pedestal and load it onto a cart… and we were stopped. Arkos

Kaiaphon came running up to us with all his servants and guards. He demanded we leave the statue in its place, or else his family would cut off funding to the Thenoan League.

"In the end, Dioscouro made a compromise. He would leave the statue in its place, but the doors would be barred shut, and no one could enter and see it."

Arkos Kaiaphon was the richest man in Thénai, a banker, mercantilist and clothier who had fingers throughout cities all along the sea. Why would Arkos demand the statue be preserved?

"Perhaps," Khloë told Phalco, "I do not know this city nearly as well as I think."

THE HIGH GROTTO

Geon sat there with the Maid of Prophecy, and as night fell, the wind had a deathly chill. The mountain air was thin, and difficult to breathe, but Geon felt more comfortable here, far from the wars and conflicts that raged in the land below.

Geon rubbed his arms together in the hope of keeping warm. The Maid of Prophecy had wrapped a cloak around her shoulders, but there was no cloak for Geon. As the light waned, his own body replaced the sun with a dull white glow. In the darkness, the blue starlight of his halo was as visible as ever, and glinted in the dark waters of the grotto.

He would not throw the Spear and Shield of Pegara in those waters. He would not die. He still had a mission. Thénai had enemies, both "within" and "without."

"I have told you much," the Maid said, "but you must hurry quickly away, tomorrow morn. My master has turned against you. That is the reason Axander was raised… to defeat you."

"Axander?" Geon said.

"I have said too much!" The Maid blushed.

The Maid of Prophecy's master was the Oracle, a woman of great wisdom and sorcerous powers. Had she raised another hero, besides Theron? Had she called upon another, merely for the sake of defeating Geon?

"Axander," Geon repeated. "What have I done to deserve death? What have I done to deserve the Oracle's wrath?"

"You disobeyed her," the Maid said, "and she does not look on disobedience kindly."

Not long ago, Geon had faced the Oracle on her holy mount. The Oracle had demanded he abandon Thénai; she had declared the city was a lost cause. But Geon had refused. He had looked into her dark eyes, and defied her openly. He had seen her for what she was… a cruel beast.

"All because I would not betray Thénai," Geon muttered. "All because I pledged allegiance. I am a citizen! I have a duty to her. I must save her."

"The Kersicans are not its greatest threat," the Maid said. "But I'm sure you knew."

Indeed, the factions that developed within Thénai, the street violence and the division, had weakened them right as the Kersican power grew.

"The temple—" the Maid began, and then stopped herself.

"The temple? What do you mean?" In his prior life, Geon had not cared much for the staid and passionless rites of the Temple of Amara, nor the wild revelry of the Brekkonals.

"I have said too much." The Maid bit her lip. "Geon, her statue is no more…"

"What do you mean?" Geon said. The statue of Amara had been built long ago of marble and ivory. It had been considered a great wonder of the world, a prized possession of Thénai, a point of civic pride.

"Her priestesses have been killed," the Maid said. "The southrons put them to the sword. All but one of them is dead."

The impiety of the southrons did not surprise him. But to kill priestesses outright, and lay waste to a temple, would have been unthinkable until not long ago.

"I must restore her temple," Geon began saying. "I must avenge this wrong…"

"A statue has been put in her place," the Maid continued. "The likeness of a demon. And it remains in the sanctuary to this day."

"I must— I must—" Geon had grown breathless, exasperated. Panic had overwhelmed him at the thought of the desecration. Where had this zeal come from? Where was he getting it?

"Greater threats lie within," the Maid said. "The peril is not in the temple."

"No, no, no," Geon was saying. "I must restore it."

"It is a fool's errand."

"I must! I must!"

The Maid pursed her lips, glaring slightly. "Geon, Geon. If you must… if that is what you want… then know only one survivor remains. Only one can restore the priesthood. She fled amid the carnage. She is a refugee among the Isteroi… in the city of Arctos. Her name is Herodota. The task of finding her will not be easy."

"But I will find her," Geon said. "I will restore what is Amara's. I will restore the temple. I will do what I must."

OUTSIDE BOS, NEAR THE KERSICAN LEAGUE

Taicho had been a hoplite only six months.

At age sixteen, he had come here, to the mainland of Eloesus from his home city across the sea. Far away, on the western edge of the world, was the city of Lornadion. That was where Taicho came from, but now he was marching on the front lines.

Taicho's journey had been long, and when his parents had gotten the news, they had not been happy.

Lornadion, so far away it seemed, even now, like a distant dream, had pledged allegiance to the Thenoan League. Taicho had never cared much for the motherland, and knew little about its politics.

But when the Thenoan emissary arrived in town, the archon and the Council of Elders had passed a motion. Every freeborn male of fighting age was to go aid the city of Thénai and its people. When the hoplites came for Taicho, his mother had pleaded and begged. "Thénai has nothing to do with us!" she had wept. "Why should he fight for a city all the way across the sea?"

But Taicho was here now. He could not go back. He was marching at the fore of the army, on the vanguard, toward the fortress of Bos, which the Thenoan League had recently captured and was desperate to hold.

He had marveled at the city's size when he reached the harbor. He had never seen a town so big.

Lornadion, facing the ocean, was buffeted by storms, a lonely outpost far from the motherland. Yet despite its impossibly great distance, despite the stormy seas separating it from Thénai, it had taken sides in the war. Taicho had not cared much for any of the bickering cities in the motherland, nor had his father or his mother. He had left two young siblings behind, a sister and a brother. He missed the cool sea breeze of Lornadion, far away, in the land of Dys, and wanted nothing more than to be home; but as a citizen of Lornadion he had been ordered to go. He'd been ordered to fight here… to march.

A river appeared, dark and brown as it meandered through the golden grass.

The fortress of Bos, built of red stone, guarded the bridge that marked the border of Thenoa and Kersica. The sun was harsh and glaring, and the bronze breastplate Taicho wore was stifling in the heat. He was still not quite used to heaving a heavy shield over his left hand, and gripping a spear in his right. He was not strong enough, yet, to be a hoplite, and he feared that when the time came, he would not be brave enough either. He was sixteen, far too young to join his grandparents and his uncle in the River of Souls. The underworld was not meant for the young; it was meant for the old.

Up above on Bos' battlements, on its parapets and towers, hundreds upon hundreds of hoplites and archers stood in the sun, the horsehair crests of their helmets gleaming vibrant reds, greens and blues in the daylight. The dog days of summer had passed them by, but the heat lingered, and winter was nowhere in sight.

~

The sun was setting, and Taicho and the rest of the soldiers filtered in through the vast fortress. In the center of it, amid the walls and fortifications, was a spacious yard. There, benches and tables had been set up, and in the heat of the day, some hoplites had broken bread and begun to drink. As Taicho took his seat, he noted a pall had fallen over the fortress, and up above them, the hoplites on the battlements had worried looks and pale faces. It was like they were doomed men, expecting destruction at any moment.

Perhaps, they were. The Kersican League was stronger, by far, and the warriors had more skill.

More than that, they had none of the scruples of the Thenoan League. They had betrayed their nation and asked for the aid of southrons. It was only with the southrons' help that they overcame the Thenoan League, even though the Thenoans were their fellow countrymen, their brothers. They had set aside the norms and laws of morality. They had betrayed their own kin.

Taicho wondered if that, after all, was why Lornadion decided to come to Thénai's aid. True, they had already pledged allegiance, but Thénai was on the other side of the world, and it was burning. It had been a losing battle, for certain; and yet Lornadion had set aside all its fears and concerns. It had risked everything for its erstwhile allies, sending its young men to fight for the motherland. It was unfortunate Taicho was among them. But he had a duty. He would not return in shame. He would return bearing his shield, or he would return in a bier. He would not bring dishonor on his family's name.

Across from him, eating bread and drinking the watered down wine, was one who looked even younger than him. He was dusky, darkly-complected, with a hint of red to his skin. His hair was dark and wool-like.

Eloesians were spread out, all across the sea; they had laid their tentacles in every dark corner and every far shore. Many colonists had married locals. No doubt this young hoplite was among them.

"Hello," Taicho said, and his voice cracked. He did not know what to say. He knew only that he was alone, far from family and from the village he had known and loved. He knew no one, and death was just on the horizon. He wanted to perish, if he had to, among friends. But he knew no one in this lonely outpost. When the new hoplites from Dys disembarked, they'd been separated.

Taicho was the only man from Lornadion in his regiment.

The man across from him looked up from his bread, with confusion in his eyes. Clearly, he did not want to talk. He did not want to make a new friend.

The young man, younger than even Taicho, apparently had nothing to say. Perhaps, he welcomed perishing alone, here, far from his home, far from all its comforts, far from friends, far from family. Here, on the other side of the world, Taicho would fight for a city he did not know, for a League he had never cared for. "The motherland is in trouble," the archon back home had said. Taicho had not been concerned. But he had accepted his duty.

That night, Taicho was posted on the battlements of Bos, keeping watch while other hoplites slept. Numerous torches were posted over the walls, and only the moonlight illuminated the land to the south, beyond the Kersican border. Crickets were chirping, and the air had turned cold. A brisk wind was blowing from the west, and Taicho exulted in the chilliness. The heat of the day had evaporated with the sun.

"Taicho," the hoplite standing next to him said. "That is your name, right?"

Taicho turned to face him. He could not make out anything about him; a helmet covered all but his eyes, gleaming blue in the moonlight. Perhaps, he was as inexperienced as Taicho, set about on a mission he had no concern for, a mission that had nothing to do with him.

"That is my name," he said.

"A strange one, for certain."

His name meant "hawk" in the language of the natives of Dys. For sure, it was strange to the motherlanders, but it was his name. It was who he was.

"Are you afraid, young Taicho?"

By his demeanor and the timbre of his voice, it had become

apparent this hoplite was older, perhaps the age of Taicho's father. No doubt he was a veteran, accustomed to war.

"I suppose I am," Taicho answered. "I never wanted to be here. But my father said I must. And the archon of Lornadion said so, too."

"I saw you talking to Pythio," the man said. "He is a strange young man, isn't he?"

"I don't know," Taicho said. "He wouldn't say a word."

"He hasn't said a word to anyone," the man continued. "And rumors have spread. 'He is a priest… he has taken a vow of silence.' 'He is a spy.' 'He is the true king of Isteros.' Don't spread rumors, Taicho. Promise me that."

"I won't," Taicho said. Why would he? He knew nothing of this Pythio, and though he was sullen, silent, perhaps rude, he had not said a word. Taicho wouldn't hold it against him. Weren't all the recruits quiet and afraid? Weren't they all reticent, knowing they might very well lose their lives?

"He is an outlander like you," the man said. "He is from Khazidea! And he is your age. Don't give up on him, Taicho."

"How do you know so much about me?" Taicho asked. It was uncanny. It was as if he had peered into his life and examined every dark corner.

"Why, I am the commander," he said. "Nestor Kaiaphon. I am pleased to make your acquaintance. I would be remiss if I did not learn about my soldiers."

~

At dawn, the birds began to sing. Every moment of remaining awake was a battle. But when the sun arose in a gleam of flame, filling the earth with its light, and Nestor announced their watch was over, he was glad the night—despite its dullness—had passed without incident. On his way down the stairs, to the ground level of Bos, Pythio passed him by. Taicho resolved that, one way or another, he would seek out this Pythio. He would learn about him, and he would make him his friend. Taicho would not fight or die alone. He sensed that Pythio did not want to, either.

GREAT ARCTOS ROAD, NORTH OF THENOA

Geon followed the busy road from a distance, keeping out of sight of passersby. He knew if they saw his wings and his glowing body, they'd call up an alarm.

When he had left the High Grotto, however, he'd been given a gift. Clipped to his belt was a potion. The Maid of Prophecy told him, if he imbibed, he'd return to normal for a while. She did not know how long, but this power inside him would be suppressed; his wings would vanish and the light he had emitted would disappear. As soon as he reached the town of Arctos, where Herodota, priestess of Amara, lived, he'd gulp down the potion. He would find her, and convince her to restore the priesthood. Then, she would return with the lesser priestesses, and they would sanctify the temple once more.

Geon did not know why he cared; he did not quite know what had come over him. In his life as a banker and moneychanger, he had never gone to the temple, not even on Third Night. But some strange zeal had overpowered him, a zeal he did not quite understand, and one that, quite frankly, had come from nowhere. When he heard a demon had replaced Amara in her temple, wrath had consumed him, wrath that had inexplicably blossomed in his heart, wrath which drove him forward.

Herodota alone knew Amara's rites and rituals. Only she could properly restore the priesthood and the temple.

As he passed through the woods, a good distance from the road, Geon's halo pierced the darkness, banishing the shadow from his feet. In the hollows, the sound of a woodpecker echoed, and blue and red birds flitted by him. Here, he was safe from the travelers passing down the road, safe from detection. The animals were drawn to him; they basked in his light. They did not treat him as different, or as aberrant. They treated him like he was a natural part of the world, even a welcome part of it.

The trees peeled away into a meadow, and there Geon heard a loud gasp.

A man lay there, crumpled, with two arrows piercing his side. He was bleeding. He was groaning wordlessly, unable to speak or call for help. He was on the verge of death; Geon could sense it. If Geon left him just moments longer, he would pass on into the underworld.

Geon walked over, and as the light of his body reflected in the man's eyes, he screamed wildly and flailed his arms, overcome with fear. Geon had added terror to the man's agony, but still he approached, wanting to help, though he did not know how. His wings seemed to stretch out of their own accord as he knelt beside the wounded man. He lifted his hands and moved his fingers toward the wounds. He was not a physician. He would likely do more harm than good.

The man's eyes had turned black like marbles. His screams had turned guttural, yet still, he was too weak to bat away Geon's hands.

As Geon pressed his fingers on the wounds, light seemed to grow around them, a cold white flame. The arrows began to loosen; the man's skin seemed to stretch and to redden. The arrowheads fell out, the bleeding ceased, and the wound sealed.

The man gasped, as if his life and strength had returned. He sat up and looked at Geon with wide brown eyes. "Who are you?" he began to babble. "*What* are you?"

What was Geon? He was not entirely sure, but he was not human, not anymore.

"Who did this to you?" Geon asked.

"Bandits…" the man said. "And my friend left me for

dead."

"Go," Geon said. "Return. Live your life. And be careful next time."

The man scurried away, healed and cured, his life saved.

Somehow, it had been Geon's doing. Somehow, the power living inside him had mended those wounds and saved that man's life. Phillipidēs had been given great strength and bravery, Helēmon a sword of fire. Was this his gift? Was this his calling? He never wanted to be a hero, but a hero's life had chosen him. He would use his powers as well as he could. But he knew he would never be accepted, not in Thénai, not anywhere.

~

A river appeared, coursing through the hills and woods, fresh and blue against the dry shrubland. Villages had begun to pop up every which way, and avoiding human contact became a difficult proposition. Dodging through woods and hurrying past roads and paths at opportune moments, Geon did his best to hide himself. Not even the Isteroi, the lowest of Eloesians, would treat him as anything more than a monster to be feared. No, they would pray and call upon the heroes of old to save them. Geon was no longer of this world; he was transforming each moment, each hour, each day. His light was growing, and his radiance seemed to intensify. Despite the Spear and Shield of Pegara, one day, it would consume him; he was sure of it. Whatever lived inside him was far too strong for a human body. Soon, it would devour him whole.

Where woods did not predominate, vast swaths of farmland were being tended. The year was late, and the harvest was almost at hand. Fields of golden wheat stretched for miles, and where wheat did not grow, rows of beans and legumes contrasted, green against the black earth. On hills and in fields, pastures contained the dwelling places of thousands upon thousands of cattle, sheep and pigs. The folk of the Isteros valley were not wise philosophers or great artists, but they certainly ate well, and they knew how to tend the soil.

The forests had disappeared altogether, and hiding had become a vastly more difficult proposition. Geon did his best to avoid farmhands, working the fields, but could not escape the occasional look of terror, or frequent flight of an onlooker. No doubt, word would spread that a monster from a strange realm was walking among them, spreading fear and panic among the Isteroi. Frequently, Geon had to resist the temptation to gulp down the vial of poison. The Maid of Prophecy had warned him, it would only last a little while. He would never go back to who he was, truly. He would never regain his humanity. He would never find the acceptance of Eloesians again. He was changed.

He was darting through a wheat field one day, hoping to avoid the looks of the farmhands, when he tripped and went flying. His wings caught him in mid-air, and settled him gently to the earth.

He turned and saw the wreckage of a chariot wheel, and a woman groaning. A bushel full of apples was in her hand, but it had overturned and spilled much of its cargo.

Not far away, farmhands were working, but they had taken no notice of him. Geon knew he should leave her there, but he found himself walking over her way.

She was sprawled out on the ground, clearly with broken bones. Her hair was red and her eyes were green, the color of ivy. She was an Isteroi if Geon had ever seen one.

"My good woman," Geon said. "Are you all right?"

What did he think? Of course, she wasn't. And moreover, by the way she didn't speak, by the way she didn't call for help, it was clear she had stolen this bushel full of apples, then raced away on a chariot. Her horses had broken free; they were nowhere to be seen. She was trapped, injured, and caught; but Geon still wanted to help her.

"What are you?" she said. "*Who* are you?"

"My good woman," he said, "I'm not entirely sure what I am."

She was immobile. She tried to move her arms, but quickly gave up after a little pain.

Geon stooped over beside her.

"I… I am sorry…"

"What are you sorry for?" Geon asked, but as he expected, she didn't answer.

He stretched out his hand, and white flame coursed around them, a gleaming of star-fire. He heard bones snap together, and then, the woman exhale. She drew in a deep breath and sat up. "Oh," she said, with tears in her eyes, "thank you."

She stood up and began to throw the apples back inside the bushel, muttering "thank you," all the way.

When she had gathered them all inside, she hurried back the way she came, back to the farmhands, back to the farmers' fields.

Onward and onward Geon went, through the farmers' fields, as the towns of the Isteroi valley grew in size, as fortresses and watchtowers appeared on hilltops. Soon, it would be impossible to hide who he was; it would be impossible to hide what he was becoming.

HIGH CITY, THÉNAI

Those poor souls.

Khloë looked down on the red roofs of the city below her. Thousands of citizens returned to their homes each day, most finding little more than burnt rubble. The walls were full of archers and hoplites, and the City Square had been turned into a military camp. In the harbor, ships poured in from tributary cities all across the Middle Sea, full of brave young men about to risk their lives for the motherland. Thénai was not what it used to be. Life had grown harder, and food was scarcer. But what Khloë truly dreaded lay behind her, not below her: the Temple of Amara, sealed shut, kept completely closed to the public thanks to the urging of the Kaiaphons.

The Kaiaphons, wealthy merchants and clothiers, were the Thenoan version of royalty, and yet, Khloë began to suspect they were Old Believers, worshiping the ancient gods. That was why they demanded the statue remain in place, hidden behind the oaken doors of the temple. And Dioscouro, archon of Thénai, could not remove it without risking the Kaiaphons' silver and gold.

The bells in the House of the Archon began to ring. The Council of War was called, and for better or worse, Khloë was a member. She had to do her best to give the Thenoan League advice, though she had lost trust in so many, and questioned everyone and everything.

~

The council of war convened in the house's courtyard. Amid the babbling fountains and the bright sun, Khloë took shelter in one of the porticoes, hoping to be an observer and nothing more.

Dioscouro strode forward in his chiton and blue sash. His

hair was silver in the light of the day. He seemed to have grown older over these days and weeks, and worry wrinkles marred his once fresh face. The city of Thénai had been rescued from utter destruction, but the League's position remained perilous. Though the Free and Democratic Armies grew in number each day, Kersica's army was greater and better skilled.

"Friends and countrymen," Dioscouro said, "we have a decision before us, and one we may not take lightly."

Every day, it seemed, there was a decision that was life or death. Where shall we attack next? Where shall we get our food? Which color should the drapes in the House of the Archon be?

"King Gygax has declared Tharta's neutrality in the war between the leagues," Dioscouro said. "We have an opportunity to turn them against the Kersicans."

Khloë had heard this tripe before. The Thartans would do no such thing.

"Amara will it, we will win them over," Dioscouro continued, and in a rage Khloë barged over.

"You speak of the goddess!" Khloë said. "And yet her sanctuary is defiled! Her statue was bashed to pieces, and now a monstrosity stands in its place! You refuse to remove it! You refuse to destroy it! How much gold and silver is worth impiety? Even now, the people march in the streets in anger! Do not ever speak of the goddess again, Dioscouro. You are unworthy of her!"

For a while, a hush fell over the courtyard, and neither the demiarchs nor the delegates from the tributary cities spoke. Dioscouro was gawking at her, but she regretted nothing. She did not regret a single word. It had been a long time coming, and the outrage had endured far too long.

"What is she speaking of?" said Gaion, a representative of the city of Bregantion. "What is the meaning of it? Is it true? Another god is honored in her temple?"

"Not a god!" Khloë shouted. "A monster! The people told me all about it! Old Dio tried to keep it from me… but beggars and carpenters, merchants and sailors… they all knew! They all knew! What Dioscouro did isn't as much a secret as he thinks. The temple remains defiled and he won't lift a finger."

Delegates of the tributary cities began to shout. Many of the demiarchs, who represented the home city, knew all about what lay within the temple doors, but foreigners were often more pious than those in the mainland. As the anger spilled forth, Khloë smiled at what she had done. Dioscouro would have a difficult time overcoming this. Was this the end of his designs? How much was Kaiaphon money worth to him? Khloë would soon find out.

"You must remove it at once!" shouted a woman she knew as Pelagia. "Or else, the city of Floridion withdraws all its support, and sends our men home."

"Quiet, quiet." Dioscouro was out of his element, unable to quell the anger, unable to quiet the storm. The rage of the Council of War was building by the second. "There is money—"

"No money is worth impiety!" Pelagia shouted. "You have brought a curse down upon us… upon our city, upon our league, and upon the heads of every man and woman standing here!"

Those who lived in the colonies were notoriously pious, and some would say simple. Scholars and wise men in Thénai largely did not believe the gods intervened directly in human affairs, and in truth, neither did Khloë, but more often than not, colonists retained the ancient beliefs and fears in the divine. To them, the city of Thénai depended utterly on the mercy and wiles of Amara. To them, what Dioscouro had done was more than a sacrilege: it was a true and present danger, risking the fortunes of the Thenoan League in a practical way.

"Open the temple doors!" shouted one of the delegates. "Or else the city of Skythos revokes its membership in the League, and we shall cease paying tribute."

Now, there was nothing Dioscouro could do. He glanced at Khloë with a look of annoyance, and bit his lip. Surely, he was counting silver and gold, how much money he would lose, as he stood there. At last, he spoke. "So be it. Come with me."

Nothing was worth the cost of losing Thénai's allies, the tributary cities which paid each year into the League's treasury and sent their young men, by the thousand, to die for its cause.

~

The sun was setting over the sea, and the sky was painted in red and bronze colors as Dioscouro and the two-hundred-member Council of War stood before the temple. The High City was cleared and empty, for fear of riots. The law courts, usually busy with the shouting of magistrates, were silent. And a pall had settled over the Council of War, and over Khloë's heart. Dread filled her as the form of Phalco and a few other bodyguards approached the sealed temple doors. They had left their swords and shields behind them. They laid their hands on the great wooden bar and began to heave it.

As they groaned, Dioscouro looked back at the Council of War behind him, as if he were expecting someone. Khloë saw that his hands were trembling. They were all afraid. Why were they afraid?

The wooden bar fell from its place, and the doors began to swing from their hinges with a loud creak. As light filled the sanctuary, bugs and scorpions scurried away into dark corners. In the gold light of dusk, the dim form of the Old God appeared, wreathed in shadow. The contours of its three heads and its scorpion-like body were black against the light. Khloë found herself stepping backward, trying to put distance between her and the bronze likeness.

The Council of War did not erupt in rage; they were as silent as they were still, frozen in place. Perhaps, they were as afraid as Khloë was. Perhaps, they dreaded what would occur if they truly removed the statue and melted it down into bronze.

Shouting echoed across the High City. Dioscouro turned back.

"My lords! My lords!"

Khloë turned toward the ramp that led to the High City. A guard was running toward them, still in armor.

"Your Excellency! Archon! There is an emergency!" He was breathless.

"What is it?" Dioscouro's voice was quiet, faint.

"Riots! Riots!" the guard was shouting. "A riot in Potters' Street... we are all in danger."

A riot in Potters' Street might take precedence in a different time, but not when that monstrosity was leering at them from the shadows of the temple. As soon as it was melted into ingots, they, and the whole of the city, could breathe easy once more. But now, it cast its long shadows, wreathed in blackness, and disquiet exuded all over the Council of War.

"We must quell the riot," Dioscouro said. "We shall remove this *thing* from its place later."

"No!" Pelagia shouted. "No! No! No!" She sounded hysterical, like a madwoman, as if she had forgotten how to speak any other word. "No! No! No! We must remove this at once!"

At her words, others began to shout back, and soon a great new quarrel erupted. Gaion punched another demiarch and another grabbed Dioscouro by the shoulders. As violence engulfed the Council of War, Khloë began to fall backward, looking upon the monstrous statue all the while. She felt like it was looking at her, like it was peering into her heart and finding her wanting, like the eyes from its three heads were not of bronze but portals into another world.

She turned and fled, not knowing where she could go, not knowing where she would hide.

BOS, KERSICAN AND THENOAN BORDER

Taicho had watched the battlements of Bos for seven nights when, the following morning, reports began to spread.

A Kersican army was on the move, fourteen-thousand strong, and at their head was a man named Axander. That was the rumor that spread through the barracks, but Taicho fell asleep anyway on his cot. He still could not acquaint himself with the night watch. Mankind was not a creature of the nighttime, but of the day. He had spent the past week in constant exhaustion, unable to function.

He awoke to alarm bells ringing and loud shouts. Young hoplites, still in their bedclothes, were scrambling to and fro around them, dressing themselves and preparing. Battle was just ahead of them. It would be their greatest, and perhaps the last, test of their lives.

Terror banished Taicho's exhaustion, and he quickly ran from room to room, dressing himself in his breastplate and his bronze greaves. At last he took the helmet, forged of bronze, with a bright horsehair crest of red, and said something not unlike a prayer, for the sake of his mother and of his father, a world away in the town of Lornadion beside the sea. In all likelihood, they would never see him again. Their son would perish for a city he did not know. Their son would die for the motherland.

He fixed the helmet to his head. It was difficult to see, but it would cushion his head against blows. He asked whatever god or spirit would listen for his survival, that they would guide his spear hand, and protect him from the enemy.

Up on the battlements, he could see the vast fields south of the border, beyond the river. In the distance, thousands of dark shapes had formed a black mass, moving towards them. Thousands upon thousands of Kersicans marched, and beyond them, Taicho made out the lumbering shapes of catapults and ballistae. They were well prepared, and they intended to take Bos, one way or the other.

"*Ai Athra!*" the hoplite next to him snapped to attention and put his left hand over his heart.

Taicho peered over and made out, through the shadows of his helmet, the face of Pythio. He was almost certain of the young man's identity. Taicho had striven to fight and risk death next to a friend. He supposed this was as close as he would come. He would battle the Kersicans by Pythio's side. It did little for Taicho's nerves, and he wanted nothing more than to break rank and flee. Pythio would not talk to Taicho, or anyone; but he would fight alongside his fellow soldiers, and what greater honor was there?

"Save me, Alabastros, king of the gods," Taicho muttered under his breath. "Save me… save me… I am far too young to die."

GREAT ARCTOS ROAD, ISTEROI KINGDOM

Geon ascended a hill, and below him, many fathoms away, on either side of the river, the stone walls of Arctos appeared, stretching in a great circle. Smoke arose from the dwelling places, and far away, the road leading into its gates were packed with horses, riders, carts and chariots. The people of Thénai, back home, often mocked the Isteroi as barbarians and savages. But the town of Arctos, even from this distance, was vast in size, and its warriors were hardy. How many times had Thénai been burnt and rebuilt? How many times had it fallen? The walls of Arctos were sturdy and tall, built of gray stone, full of turrets and towers. The Isteroi were not the ignorant outsiders that Thénai claimed. Their accents were strange, and their hair was often red, but they were not savages by any means.

From his belt, Geon unclipped the jar that the Maid of Prophecy had given him. He removed the leaden cap, and a foul smell emanated from it. The liquid was dark, the color of blood, and had a metallic scent to it. He wondered what was inside it, and why it would stop his transformation.

He began to gulp it down. It was syrupy, thick and viscous, and sickening in its salty, putrid taste. He felt himself change; the light glowing from inside his hands and feet began to fade. His body grew heavy. He could no longer feel his wings.

And in a flash, he grew angry at what he had done. Why was he here? Why had he risked everything for the sake of the goddess and this so-called priesthood? How much danger was he walking into? The cause was foolish! He would return to Thénai. He would find his old life again. Perhaps, his old friend Dismos had stuck around. How many glasses of wine had they drunk together on the harbor? How many times had they dreamed of going into business together?

Geon turned back, toward the road, toward the city that was truly his home. It embarrassed him that he was even here, among these savage Isteroi, among these red-headed barbarians of little education and less culture. As he approached the Great Arctos Road, he turned up his nose at them. They were ignorant. They were not Eloesians at all.

And soon, very soon, Geon would be back home.

THE FOX AND THE HARE

A FABLE

One day a fox was pursuing a hare through the woods. At last, he caught up with the hare, but just as he was about to bite, the hare fell into an iron trap, breaking its foot and opening up a dolorous wound.

"Help me!" the hare said. "The hunters are here, and they want you just as much as me!"

But the fox laughed. "They will want no such thing!"

He devoured the hare and went about his way, licking his lips. As he drew near his den, a trap sprung, but there was no one to help him get away. That evening, the hunters found him, and took him away to make a pelt.

—Amalchio

CITY SQUARE, THÉNAI

Khloë, together with her retinue, had begun to make her way to Potters' Street in the light of dusk. Dioscouro had promised both her and the rest of the Council of War that the monstrosity in the temple would be melted down the next day. For now, pressing concerns had emerged, and Khloë—flanked at each side by bodyguards, and joined by the Politarch of Public Order—was making her way to the site of the riot.

Potters' Street had a storied history. In an earlier era, it had been the focus of pottery production, shipping its amphorae, vessels and containers to every colony across the sea. Potters' Street had made Thénai famous, but in recent times it had lost much of its glory. Now, it was visited by the dissolute and disreputable. There was a brothel on each of its corners, and pottery production had—by necessity—moved elsewhere, closer to the harbor. What this riot was about, Khloë could only imagine. Many had lost their homes, and surely many of those dens of ill repute had been scorched to rubble as well.

She knew she'd gotten close to Potters' District when the shouting began to rise above the city's din. Night had almost fallen over Thénai but these rioters were still on the streets, still shouting, still making a nuisance of themselves.

The streets opened into a broad thoroughfare. All throughout, half-finished buildings lay bare, abandoned by the workmen for the day. Timber frames and partially dug foundations predominated. But in the distance, to Khloe's left, a way down the street, a motley mob had assembled, men, women and children shouting and screaming, some bearing torches, some brandishing daggers.

Khloë pointed to them and, with her retinue, approached

the scene of the commotion. "What is the meaning of this?" she shouted, but her voice did not carry above the crowd.

"We demand the release of Chillos!" Their chant had become audible against the silence of the night. "We demand the release of Chillos!"

Beyond them, smoke was rising. Perhaps, the mob had set fire to one of Thénai's buildings. A riot was never a noble thing, no matter the participants' degree of self-righteousness. There was no excuse for destroying property and vandalizing the city, especially when it was trying to recover. The city remained on a precipice; even now, it was attempting to recover from the vast destruction that had been visited upon it. Countless thousands had died, and many more driven from their homes; and the barbaric Kersicans had left bodies to rot, causing a swarm of flesh flies to maim and disfigure the survivors.

As Khloë, her guards, and the politarch drew near, the crowd stopped their shouting, and stood there, glaring.

"What is the meaning of this?" Khloë said.

"Why don't you tell us?" a woman hissed. "Poor Chillos! Poor Chillos! They took him…"

Others began to shout. "I'll kill him!" a man screamed. "I'll kill that Lysander!"

Lysander, one of the highest ranking commanders, controlled a battalion of hoplites that kept public order. Even when the city was at peace, the Thirty-Sixth Battalion remained within the city walls, carrying out arrests on behalf of the archon, seizing suspected murderers and thieves. Lysander was well loved by everyone, a highly respected military commander in addition to a civic officer. Yet clearly, this mob thought he had done wrong.

"Who is this Chillos?" Khloë said. "What are you speaking of?"

Out of the mob the form of a man and woman emerged,

dressed in dull gray clothing.

"He was my boy," the woman said. "And now he is gone. Lysander took him."

"He took him? Why?" Khloë said.

"He took a bit of bread!" Chillos' father answered. "A bit of bread, from a merchant stall! And Lysander's thugs seized him and dragged him away. What man takes a boy when he steals bread? It was just bread! And now he is in the city jail! The jail, they say! The jail. I swear, I'll kill that Lysander! I'll wring his neck."

Indeed, it was strange that such a harsh punishment was carried out for theft, especially against a young boy. It warranted some investigation.

"I will see what I can do," Khloë said. "I will see why Lysander's taken him."

"Thank you," Chillos' mother said with tears in her eyes. "Thank you, amazon… do not disappoint me."

~

Khloë ordered her bodyguard and the Politarch of Public Order to go their separate ways. She would investigate this matter alone. For certain, it was odd. Jail was not a regular punishment for bread theft, even for an adult man. At most, a fine was levied, and for a repeat thief, a heavier fine. To set an adult in prison, with poor living quarters and meager fare, required much harsher crimes. To do such a thing to a young boy was unthinkable, and certainly not for bread theft.

The siege had ruined many citizens of Thénai, and made them desperate. The food pouring in from the colonies was not enough, and hunger stalked the city's streets like a dark huntress. There were not enough provisions for everyone, and thieves abounded.

Khloë made her way toward the harbor. The sun had set, and darkness was beginning to creep over the sky. Her sabers were always by her side, but an unnerved feeling had settled over her, and she wondered if a force was preying through the city, a force she could not contend with. The street lamps offered only minimal illumination. The curfew was in force, and none could travel the city without risk of arrest, but many were willing to press their luck. The street to the harbor, however, was completely empty. Khloë was alone; or was she?

~

City Prison was a dark-bricked building, surrounded by a high fence, but the guards recognized Khloë instantly and let her by. Here, violent criminals were held for trial… murderers, traitors and insurrectionists were housed in its damp, disease-ridden cells, fed a diet of hard bread and tasteless water as they wasted away. It was no place for a common thief. It was certainly not a place for a child.

The prison warden was in the vestibule. A ring of keys jingled at his side whenever he walked. He was a portly man, wide and tall, and wore a leather jerkin over his chest. In the corner, a pair of guards, off-shift, rolled dice at a table. Only the oil lamp where they sat offered any illumination.

The prison warden bowed. "My lady," he said. "An honor to meet you."

What a difference it was from the colonies. Khloë was an amazon, but here, she was treated like the member of the governing elite she was. In Thenoans' eyes, or at least most of them, Khloë the Amazon was a noble, one of the ruling class.

"A pleasure," Khloë said. "I have a question."

The prison warden looked at her blankly.

"A boy…" Khloë's nerves were all wound up. "A boy name Chillos…"

"There are three-thousand in City Prison," he said. "Three-thousand awaiting their sentences. Perhaps, a hundred with that very name, if not more."

"Chillos of Potters' Street," Khloë said. "A young boy! Surely, you don't have many children locked up here, in City Prison. Else, I'll have to tell the House of Assembly."

But when had the House of Assembly ever fixed a problem? When had the archon ever been bothered to care about anything besides the war?

The prison warden led her to a room off the side of the vestibule. There, a lamp was burning, and a logbook had been set out. Each page contained hundreds of names and more writing.

The prison warden took a seat and began paging through the logbook. He began muttering to himself. "Chiander… Choros… ah, here. Chillos. Thirteen years old. Potters' Street."

The prison warden got up and beckoned Khloë to follow.

~

Clutching an oil lamp in his hands, the prison warden led her down corridors of rough flagstone. Voices called out at them as they passed by cells full of criminals. Some whistled at Khloë, who was garbed—as usual—in a loose fitting red dress.

She had begun to wonder if the living quarters were too rough, even for a prison. Perhaps, she would take it up with the Politarch of Public Health or the archon himself.

A creeping feeling had come over her; she knew, behind each black hole and cell door, there were numerous eyes watching her, men, women, traitors, murderers and vandals. This was no place for a child. This was no place for anyone, besides the worst of the worst.

The network of hallways came to an end at a dark passageway. Beyond it lay stairs, chipped away and crudely-chiseled.

"There is another level?" Khloë cried, incredulous.

"Yes," the prison warden said. "In the dungeon, we keep the worst of offenders."

"And Chillos is there?" Khloë snapped, aghast.

"I don't make the rules," the prison warden said.

But who did? That would be the first thing to find out.

~

The "dungeon," as the prison warden called it, was vast and almost completely pitch black. The prison warden's oil lamp was like a beacon in the midst of a dark expanse. Behind the doors of cells, Khloë heard a madman cackling, and another grunting like a beast.

Soon, it became evident that Khloë was splashing through water. Water, about an inch up to her sandal, had the unmistakable scent of the sea.

"Sorry, my lady," the prison warden said. "We are so far below ground, a bit of moisture is inevitable."

Not even a murderer deserved to live in this place, not even an insurrectionist or a traitor. Water from the sea was dripping in, perhaps from cracks in the foundation. How quickly would one take ill? A sentence here meant death.

"Here he is," the prison warden said. The dungeon was so dark she couldn't see the door. "He was housed with Thestas."

Khloë gasped. Thestas? Thestas? It was impossible. Thestas had attempted an insurrection at the height of the Kersican siege, attempting to storm the city and slay the archon on behalf of the pacifists. And, somehow, a thirteen-year-old bread thief had been housed with him.

The prison warden fiddled with his keys and moments later, the rusty hinge of a door creaked. The prison warden entered and Khloë followed after.

The light of the oil lamp reflected gold in a man's eyes. His beard had grown wild and untamed in all these months in prison. His ribs were showing on his chest, and his hands and legs were chained to the cell's walls. He was growling like an animal. There was a crazed look to him.

"Thestas," the prison warden said. "Where is Chillos?"

Thestas stopped his growling and began to laugh, at first a light chuckle and then a cackle. "They took him," he said. "They took him! They took him!"

The boy was nowhere to be found.

GREAT ARCTOS ROAD

Geon was headed back home, toward Thénai and the life he had left behind. It was night when his skin, once more, began to glow.

The travelers beside him screamed and fell back.

He keeled over and began to retch. In a burst of light, the blue halo seared its way back into existence. In a flash, his wings emerged once more.

A merchant drew his sword. "Back, monster!" he screamed. Others began to run.

Geon turned and fled off road. The mixture he'd drunk had lost its potency, and now, as he sprinted away, shame filled him at what he had done. He had turned his back on the holy temple, on Amara's priesthood, and for what gain? He had to find her, and now—without that foul potion—he would have to do so undisguised, with every bit of him revealed.

As he ventured back toward Arctos, it dawned on him: his motivations were not his own. They were propelling him forward. The poison he'd drunk had not just removed his outward glory, but his inner drive. Geon was no longer Geon. He had changed. Something else dwelt inside him, something terrible and powerful. He was not himself, and he never would be himself again.

~

Late at night, he ascended a hill and saw the lights and smoke of the city of Arctos below him. It was built on either side of the Ister River. The homes and buildings of Arctos were towering in size, almost as high as the wall, and in the center was an artificial High City, built of dirt, with a fortress upon it. Geon felt like he had seen this before.

He recalled that he had—just in a different form, before his poison had worn him away.

Even after dark, the city was alive. The gates were open. Some were still entering. It was as good a time as any. Would they accept Geon? He knew they wouldn't. But what else could he do, except try?

As he drew near the gate, a few late-night travelers fell back from him, screaming, and bolted in the opposite direction, into the fields. Guards came running out, brandishing spears and shields. Their faces were ashen, but they remained in place, frozen there—out of duty or out of fear, he had no idea.

"I mean you no harm," Geon said. "I truly don't." He didn't know what to say. "I am looking for a priestess. She is a refugee. Her name is Herodota. She is the only one I want."

"Get back!" The guard shouted, but his words came out a strained squeak. "Get back, demon! Flee from here! Flee and do not return!"

"Herodota… she is the only one I want," Geon said. "I must speak to her."

"Get back, monster!" another guard screamed. "We protect all in Isteros. Even refugees. Herodota will be safe from you."

"I mean no one any harm," Geon said, but the guards began to charge him. A mob of them swarmed him, but he blocked each blow and strike with his shield.

He did not want to hurt them. They did not understand. They did not know he was far from a monster. They did not understand his mission.

The winds carried him, and he half glided, half ran away, away from Arctos, away from the city, into the cool of the outlying hills.

BOS, KERSICAN AND THENOAN BORDER

For hours, the Kersican army had remained still. The soldiers and siege engines were dark outlines against the setting sun, mere shadows in the dim illumination of twilight, but all day they had kept in place. The knot in Taicho's gut, however, had only grown and twisted into new, more gruesome shapes. He almost wished the battle had begun already, and he could face all its attendant dangers head-on. For hours, he had stood here, locked shield in shield with Pythio according to his training, with a sword in his right hand. No one spoke or murmured. It seemed fear had fallen over everyone. Death lurked on the horizon. How could a motley band of young men, with no training, from colonies across the sea, possibly defeat the well-trained Kersicans? They were, and always had been, the greatest of the warriors of the motherland.

Over the long stretch of time, Taicho had heard Pythio muttering prayers under his breath. Some words he recognized; others, he did not. The commander of Bos had said Pythio was from a colony in Khazidea, a mysterious land on the edge of the Southern World. Yet Pythio did not let anyone get close to him. He did not let anyone ask questions. He was intensely private, and he kept to himself.

Out of the haze of the hot sun, a dark figure distinguished itself from the army. It was walking toward them.

Eventually, Taicho recognized the form of a man, dressed lightly, not in a bronze breastplate but in a light tunic and short leggings. His brown hair was held up in a headband. A bag of stones was clipped to his belt. In his left hand was a sword, in his right a sling.

For an emissary of the Kersican army, he was an odd

figurehead, not dressed according to military tradition. Kersican hoplites were fond of wearing red capes; in fact, it was their symbol. He was dressed like a commoner, but had weapons like a man of war.

Nestor, commander of Bos, a few rows down from Taicho, greeted him with a shout. "Who goes there?" he said. "What is the meaning of this?"

"Axander is my name!" he shouted. "And I come to bring you a message. We, the army, must pass through! You are not our targets! We are not soldiers of Kersica, but hunters, and we chase a mighty prey!"

"The border is closed!" Nestor shouted back at him. "None may enter, and none may go! That is the decree of the archon!"

Did this Axander really expect them to believe him? Did he really expect them to think an animal required a dozen siege engines to defeat?

"You do not believe me!" Axander answered. "And you must answer for it! A monster is in your midst! A creature from another realm, and it will take an army to defeat him! He will turn his wiles to you, if you do not let us through!"

"The border is shut!" Nestor shouted. "The way is closed! Go find another way to fight this creature! You must think Thenoans are fools!"

Axander turned and walked back to his army. Soon he had become a dark silhouette, a black spot against a gold canvas. Then horns blew, and the army began to march. The battle was upon them. Here, Taicho would fight alongside Pythio. Here, he would fight, across the world from his home, for a city he did not know, all for the sake of the motherland. Taicho did not want to die for the Thenoan League. He did not want to die at all. But that was what the gods in holy heaven had decided.

The assault came upon them suddenly. From a distance, the catapults began flinging mighty boulders, which shook the foundations of the walls whenever they struck, and sent hoplites tumbling to their feet. In a blitz, ladders began to fall upon the parapets, and Kersicans did their best to scale them. Thenoans answered with vats of boiling water and oil, scalding them as they tried to ascend. But as boulders fell with regularity, bits of the wall began to crumble, and the fortress was shaken.

For three days and three nights they fought, with hundreds dying.

On the morning of the fourth day, a boulder struck the gate of Bos, killing dozens in a single strike.

The forces of Axander began to push through. Bit by bit, the resistance was crumbling.

It was as Taicho long expected; he would die here, far from home, far from Lornadion, far from mother and father and his siblings, far from his childhood friends. Only his memory would remain behind: a young man who left his home, and perished for a cause he never quite believed in. In a pauper's grave he would be buried, without mark or sigil. In time, even his memory would perish from the earth.

HIGH CITY, THÉNAI

A great quarrel had broken out the night of the riot, and when Khloë returned the doors of the temple had shut once more, for fear of destruction. Delegates from tributary cities and demiarchs had been consumed with open violence, and many colonies announced their withdrawal of support from the Thenoan League.

Khloë had been consumed with logistics, of this city or that city and how much each had contributed to the Thenoan League's cause. She had forgotten about the matter of Chillos and the prison, but one morning, as she walked out onto the ground of the High City, she remembered.

Birds were singing and the morning air was fresh and crisp. The sun was shining and the sky was a bright blue. It was a marked contrast with the dark dampness of City Prison, where countless thousands wasted away, eagerly awaiting death.

She remembered poor Chillos, his sobbing mother, his angry father. She remembered the horror she'd felt that night, the sick feeling in her gut as she descended into the dungeon where no human being deserved to be held, much less a bread thief, much less a child.

And then she recalled the words of the insurrectionist Thestas. "They" had taken him. Who, indeed, were "they?"

The bells rang, summoning the Council of War, but Khloë ignored it. She had skipped those fruitless meetings before. Why not again?

Leaving the shouting of the magistrates behind her, she began to descend the High City, toward the streets below.

~

Life had truly begun to return to Thénai.

In City Square, merchant stalls crowded out the sun, and the shouting of vendors and their buyers formed a deafening cacophony. A dog ran by Khloë and a child came rushing past her at a sprint. Pigeons waddled among the hive of humanity, pecking and searching for crumbs. Each day, refugees returned to their homes by the thousands, but many more refugees were coming too, refugees who had never lived in Thénai before. Cities and towns across the Thenoan League were giving up their best and brightest for the cause. The city felt itself again as Khloë passed through: a hive not just of commerce but of ideas, of art and philosophy. But she hoped, and she prayed, that they would not make their old mistakes. Their first concern was the war itself, and the city's security. They could not allow passions to get the best of them. The citizens of Thénai had to remain united. They had to cohere, or else the old divisions would spell doom.

Eventually, she reached City Prison, guarded by a high gate. The black stone of the building was made no brighter by the sun, and the main gate was like a cave mouth to the underworld. Khloë knew full well what awaited her. Thénai's City Prison would be as much a place of gloom and despair in the day as it was in the night. As she drew near the door, the sense of dread she felt was palpable, and her stomach was twisting to knots and curls. "Chillos," she found herself muttering. "Chillos. Be safe. Be safe, my child. I am coming for you…"

~

As such a high-ranking civic official, there were certain privileges for Khloë. For one, Khloë had access to every inch of Thénai's City Prison, and she could come and go as she pleased. For another, no one could say no to her. If the prison warden wouldn't tell her everything he knew, he could find himself in trouble with the magistrate.

And yet, as she approached the prison's dark doors, she knew her power was limited. For one, neither the archon Dioscouro nor any member of the Assembly knew of her concerns. This mission was hers alone. She did not think that they would care. But moreover—even though the statue had been removed from its place—she had begun to think twice about everyone she once knew. She looked at Dioscouro, Phalco and others with a wary eye. After all, they had invited in the money of the Kaiaphons, and had thought nothing of doing dealings with Old Believers. Sometimes, as she slept, she remembered the village of Bastos across the sea, of the sacrificial knives the Old Believers held, and wondered if one was ever in the hand of Dioscouro.

Her piety had gotten her into trouble before, and it was clear Dioscouro looked down on her because of it. The politicking and whispers of Thénai's elite was omnipresent, and only a fool trusted her friend, but now, Khloë's distrust of others had increased a hundredfold, and even people she had once confided in, she viewed as potential enemies.

In the dark of City Prison, Khloë knocked on the door of the prison warden. A few moments later, it opened with a creak, and the warden's pudgy face appeared in the dim lamplight.

"My good woman?" the warden said. "Ah. Khloë. I thought you would come back."

It was clear he was uncomfortable, that he did not want to see her.

"What is this about?" the warden said.

"I think you know," Khloë said. "A thirteen year old child, in a dungeon, taken. And there is only one set of keys."

"No," the warden said, "there are many sets of keys. Each guard has a pair. And moreover, you royal folk up on the High City have a copy of each."

In all her time in the Council of War and speaking in the House of Assembly, she had not seen the keys to City Prison. But it would not surprise her at all. Dioscouro was exacting and controlling; he loved power more than anything else. He wanted control over the processes of the House of Assembly, and over the duties of each politarch. Why, then, would he not seek power over each prisoner in this squalid place?

~

With a set of keys in her left hand and an oil lamp in her right, Khloë made the descent from the upper stories of the prison into the dark underworld of a ground level, which they called the "dungeon."

The jeers and whistling of the prisoners no longer bothered her; the cell doors were well made, and even without her sabers, Khloë was strong enough to land a solid punch. Khloë was not a frail human but an amazon, capable of holding her own. Even if the prisoners broke free, she would overcome them.

The stairs were slippery and uneven as she descended into the deep darkness. The oil lamp reflected on the chips and grooves of the stairs, where water and moisture had gathered. The air grew cooler and cooler as she continued, and far away, below her, the sound of cackling echoed. Madness was often the cause of dark crimes… insanity, driven by dark spirits, propelled the deranged to murder.

When she reached the cell, she saw that it was empty.

Thestas, insurrectionist, was gone.

She recalled a number of criminals had been transported to

a theater on the edge of the city for public beheading. Such public displays were limited to punishments the State wished to advertise: punishments such as insurrection and rebellion, which Thestas had been accused of. Perhaps, in the days since Khloë left, Thestas' trial had been held, and he had suffered the punishment which insurrection required.

Now, Khloë would never be able to interrogate him. She'd never know who, or what, had taken poor Chillos. Perhaps, in such poor conditions, the thirteen-year-old had taken ill, and—in embarrassment—prison officials buried him in a hasty grave outside the city. The possibilities were endless. But Thestas, and his one-time cellmate, were gone. A great injustice had been done, one which would never be answered for.

"Hey! Amazon!" The raspy voice that greeted her came from the opposing cell, on the other side of the corridor. "Have you ever seen a man disappear?" He began to giggle.

Khloë pointed her lamp toward him. She could just barely make out the reflection of dark eyes, glinting in the lamplight. He was in his cell, peering through prison bars.

"They took Thestas away!" the madman said. "They took him away! And they left me behind! Praise Amara! Praise Alabastros! Praise Nix!"

In such a dark place, mentioning the goddess of magic and secrets was anathema; it was almost inviting her presence. Khloë shuddered. She felt goose-prickles forming on her skin as she saw those eyes gazing upon her, as she wondered how many more were looking at her as well.

"*They* took him away?" Khloë said. She did not want to speak with a madman, but she supposed she had no choice. What better witness was there?

"They sawed off his chains!" the madman said. "They sawed off his chains and took him away! But Thestas wasn't happy.

He was screaming. Afraid."

"Who are they? The prison warden? Did he do it?" Khloë had begun to shake.

"They came from inside! From inside! They are like rats! Rats! Rats!" The madman began to cackle.

But despite his hysteria, Khloë wondered if it was true, if he had truly seen something. She walked back into Thestas' old cell, not sure what she would see, not sure what, exactly, would happen.

The cell was submerged in water, breaching even Khloë's sandals as she walked.

As the madman said, Thestas' chains lay on the ground, but as Khloë walked closer, the oil lamp's light filled the room, and she saw no key had been used. The metal had been crudely sawed off, and no neck-cuff was visible. Whoever had taken Thestas did not have his key. And the madman had told her *they*—whoever "they" were—had come from within the room, somehow. Yet there was no door.

Across the room, another chain lay in the water, half-submerged, also sawed in two. Was that the former chain of young Chillos? If he, too, had been taken in the same manner as Thestas, there had been no key, no official sanction from the prison warden or the leadership of City Prison.

As she walked over to the broken chain, she tripped and almost lost her sandal.

She turned and saw that it had caught on a hinge.

A trapdoor, barely visible through the water, was made to look like stone.

Khloë was still dressed in her gown, still dressed in the manner of a public official, but she had no choice. She stooped down, fumbling around for the latch. At last she laid hold of the sides of the trapdoor, and opened it.

Water came trickling downwards, into a dark and lightless

passageway below.

~

With a lamp in her left hand, she eased herself downward.

The corridor was thin and narrow, roughly hewn, and it was headed south-eastwards, away from the sea. She did not know what to expect, but she knew one thing: if she wanted to find Chillos, and bring justice to his family, if she wanted to end the unrest on Potters' Street, she had to follow this dark passageway, no matter what monsters or wraiths awaited her. If she found Chillos' captors here, underneath City Prison, she would face them head-on.

Deeper and deeper she went, half-crawling, half-walking as she made her way onward. Water dripped constantly from the ceiling above.

Eventually, she began to hear noises up above her: the stamping of horses' hooves and the sound of cart wheels. The passageway had left the solitude of the harbor and City Prison, and entered the heart of the city, where commerce and civic life had once again begun to thrive.

The passageway made a sharp upward ascent, eventually turning into stairs. Up above her, a trapdoor marked the exit. She hesitated, wondering if Chillos' kidnappers were waiting for her, swords in hand.

She took a deep breath, said a prayer, laid her hands on the trapdoor, and pushed.

Above her, the sky was clear and blue, and the sun was shining down on her. She exited the darkness and found herself at the center of a cobblestone square. Ahead was a fence, flanked by two lion statues, and beyond, the courtyard of a vast mansion. Its red roof gleamed in the sun, and its white plaster walls radiated in the brightness. Before the gate, a sign read: "The House Kaiaphon."

OUTSIDE ARCTOS, ISTEROI KINGDOM

The past days had convinced Geon he would never enter Arctos in the state he was in.

He remembered the potion which the Maid of Prophecy had given her. He no longer had it; he had drunk it, and something had come over him. His old motivations, his old goals, had returned with a vengeance.

So now, what was there for him?

He had fled the guards, who threatened to kill him. Now, he was perched upon a hill, looking down on the city below. There had to be some way to find Herodota.

She alone could restore the priesthood of Amara. She alone could restore the goddess's sanctuary. She represented an unbroken chain of priestesses before her; she knew the rites and rituals of Amara—rites and rituals which were kept secret from the public at large, and never written down. Without Herodota, the temple would remain in its defilement. The sanctuary would never return to its former state, even if the goddess's statue was replaced.

But how could he find her, in this state? How could he pluck Herodota from her hiding place? He could not fly on these wings; and he did not know where she lived. She, as a refugee, surely blended in with the others. Surely, in this foreign place, she did not wear the garb of the priestess; she did not wear her hair in braids, don face paint and her blue gown. How, out of this city of many thousands, could Geon distinguish her from the others?

Perhaps, I will have to force myself in. The guards and the folk of Isteros may hate me, but they cannot stop me.

What was a little bloodshed compared to finding Herodota and restoring the temple?

But would she listen to him in that circumstance, even in all his glory? Would she accompany a creature which had slain her friends, which had sent this city of refuge into chaos?

No. There had to be some other way to draw her out. But how, he had no idea. In the state he was in, radiant and alien to human eyes, there was no way for him to speak to others, no way for him to communicate or ask anyone. How could he possibly determine where Herodota was, let alone convince her to return to Thénai? Perhaps, the mission itself was hopeless. But Geon would not give up, not as long as he lived.

He began to walk away, up the hill, through fields of wheat, away from the city of Arctos until its walls were out of sight. Beyond him, in either direction, on either side of the River Ister, there were farm fields. Rows of golden wheat stretched into the interminable distance, mixed with cow pastures and bean patches. But beyond him, just a glimmer in the horizon, was a green spot he recognized as a forest. There, the trees would hide him and his splendor. The day was growing late. He could regroup. He could think. He could recover in silence and seclusion.

~

Night was falling over the Isteroi Kingdom when he reached the forest. The oaks and cypresses covered him, hiding his wings from sight. Amid ivy and hanging moss, in the cool of the shade, he exulted in the solitude. He stretched his wings like they'd never been stretched before.

Darkness was falling, but he was alone. He walked deeper into the woods. Squirrels and foxes peered at him from the bushes, their black eyes gleaming in the light of Geon's radiance.

Eventually, he came to a deep pool. The edge of the pool was overgrown with reeds, but nevertheless, he removed his sandals and stepped in, allowing the mud to sink around his bare toes. For the first time in days, he felt safe, relaxed, completely at ease. No farmer or city-dweller could see him. He was completely alone, save for the beasts of the wood. And beasts told no secrets.

The blue stars, so numerous they formed a halo around his head, reflected in the dark pool. But as he peered into the waters, he noted another light beside him, one he'd never seen before. The mote of white light hovered just above him, to his right, but when he looked up, there was no sign of it. He was completely alone.

He began to remove his clothing, first his tunic and then his breeches, intending to bathe. At last, he removed his underclothes and stepped into the cold waters, naked except for the light and splendor emanating from his body.

He entered the depths of the water, allowing the frigidness to wash away the stresses and worries of the day. He swam to the center of the pool.

A fox had trotted up to his discarded clothing and begun to sniff. But there was no food for it. It looked up at Geon, peering with its dark eyes.

"I am sorry, fox," Geon said. "You won't find anything in there."

For a while, the fox merely looked at Geon. Then it opened its mouth.

"I know," it said. "I haven't found a thing."

Geon gasped and swam backward.

Perhaps, he had gone mad. Perhaps, all these days, standing in the sun with little nourishment and water, his mind had begun to waste away. Foxes could not talk, nor could any animal. That much was clear.

"My lord," the fox said. "You seem perturbed about something." Though it opened its mouth, and gnashed its fangs, its tongue and lips do not move. Geon was hearing the voice merely in his own head. What if all animals had such thoughts, but no way to express them?

Beside the fox, squirrels had gathered, red squirrels, black squirrels, brown squirrels. But the fox did not hunt them down or rend them with its claws. All were transfixed, staring at Geon, not wishing to move, remaining completely still.

"What is wrong?" a black squirrel said without moving its lips.

"Nothing you can help with," Geon answered. "A lost cause… a failed mission… it's hopeless. Hopeless."

A white bird flew down onto one of the pine boughs. It blinked its pink eyes and adjusted its head as it looked at Geon this way, then that way.

He wondered if, as this transformation progressed, he'd be able to command these animals as he wished. He'd gained powers of healing, swiftness and strength. And now he could hear and speak the tongues of beasts.

"My lord," the white bird said, clutching the pine bough with its talons. "What is this lost cause of yours?"

"The city of Arctos… have you ever been to it?" Geon said.

"I do not know anything by that name," the white bird answered, "but I have gone to where those humans live. There are plentiful crumbs, but I lost my mate. A human killed her with a sling, and put her in a pot."

The speech of these animals had become commonplace to him; he no longer looked at them strangely. Yes, of course, he thought, animals saw all that went on, and though they knew much, their mouths were closed, unable to reveal their knowledge.

"Down there, in that city, a woman lives," Geon said. "Herodota. A priestess."

Did animals know what a priestess was? Would they have any idea what he spoke of?

"I am trying to find her," Geon said. "But the humans will not let me by. They are afraid of me."

"Afraid of you!" the white bird cried. "But you are so beautiful."

"That is not how they see it," Geon said.

"Herodota," the white bird said. "I will go down there. I will try to keep safe. I will do anything for you, my lord… anything at all!"

The white bird darted away through the trees, toward the hills, toward the smoke and din of Arctos. Geon wanted to stop him, but he'd flown away too quickly. What worth was there to risk his life for Geon's sake, when there was such little chance of success? How could a bird ever find Herodota? Their mouths had opened, but they remained beasts, unable to think clearly, unable to dwell on much besides danger and hunger.

The fox perked up its ears and stood on its hind legs, beginning to sniff.

In a flash, the animals began scurrying away.

Geon, naked in the pool, was wreathed only in his glory. He could sense danger coming; he could taste it in the wind, but he remained in place.

The Spear and Shield of Pegara, which checked the power growing within him and allowed him to survive, lay untended by his clothes.

Out of the trees, a man emerged. His beard was bushy and bright red. Over his wide girth he had a breastplate, and in his right hand was an axe.

"Monster!" he shouted. "I saw you in the woods. I knew them trees were glowing. I knew you were hiding inside. There is a price on your head, monster! Did you know that? A price on your head! Fifty *doukon* if I clip your wings and bring you back to Arctos."

"A price on my head!" Geon was not intimidated. "And

who will give you that silver and gold?"

"King Ydro is a rich man. So come out… come out of that pool, monster. I am a man of honor. My father was a warrior, and his father as well. Grab your weapons! I will not lay hands on an unarmed man!"

Calling Geon a "man" was a refreshing change. He had not heard that word used for himself in a long while. But though he had the form of a man, and the body of one, he had changed, and he was changing more every day. The people of Eloesus looked at his wings and his blue halo with horror and disgust, not in wonderment like the animals did.

"What is your name?" Geon said to the would-be warrior. When he peered into the man's eyes in the deep darkness, he sensed a troubled soul. He could sense this man was poor—desperate, even. He would risk his life for fifty *doukon*, for that meant he could feed his family. His wife had grown distant; his children were malnourished and often missed meals. How could he strike such a person dead?

"Andar," the man mumbled. Already, he had softened his expression. His hands had begun to tremble. Were those tears glimmering in his eyes? He had loosened the grip on his axe. At last, he lowered it. "And what is yours?"

"Geon," he answered.

"That is not the kind of name I expected. I had a friend named Geon," Andar said. "Are you from up above? Are you from somewhere else? You are not from Eloesus… you are not even of this world, are you?"

"I once was," Geon said. "I once was just like you."

Andar at last dropped the axe entirely. "I will not harm you, creature of the sky," he said. "I will not harm you, now that I have beheld you. I have never felt… I have never…"

Geon spread his wings, and his body seemed to spread

more light than ever before. Soon all was clear, the greenness of the pine trees, the untidiness of Andar's beard, the exact hue of his bronze breastplate. He had begun to untie the straps, loosening the armor until it had fallen off entirely. At last, he dropped to his knees and knit his fingers together worshipfully.

"No, no," Geon said. "Stand back up on your feet."

Andar obeyed.

Though he did not want to use this pitiful man as a tool, he had begun to wonder and to think. A bird could not find Herodota, but perhaps this Andar could. Geon did not want to burden him any further; he could sense his pain, his poverty, his affliction. But he could not restore the Temple of Amara without Herodota, and he could not draw her out of the city without another's help.

Andar was standing there, at ease, letting Geon's splendor wash over him.

"Will you do something for me, Andar?" Geon said, and his voice carried throughout the wood; it was like the voice of many, like a choir.

"Of course," Andar said. "Anything. Anything at all, for you, my lord."

"A woman is in your town," Geon said. "A woman from Thénai."

"Damned refugees," Andar mumbled, then stopped himself, as if he'd said something profane.

"Her name is Herodota," Geon said. "She was once a priestess. Bring her to me, Andar, and your reward will be great."

He had spoken a lie; Geon had no reward for Andar, no way of paying him back. He had no silver and gold, no food or precious gifts to give him. But what was a little deception compared to restoring the Temple of Amara and the goddess's priesthood?

"I will do as you say," Andar said, and despite himself fell to his knees once more, clasping his hands together. "I will do anything you say.”

He stood back up and grabbed his breastplate and axe, then hurried off into the night, away from the forest, away from Geon, away from Geon's glory.

~

At the edge of the pond, Geon donned his clothing once more. He would wait here. Andar, his human servant, would bring him what he wanted. He was sure of it. He could not go to Herodota, but Herodota could go to him.

CITY SQUARE, THÉNAI

Underneath the street of the House Kaiaphon was an underworld, a dark passageway stretching into City Prison. The memory echoed in Khloë's mind as she followed the archon Dioscouro to the House of Assembly. She could not help but dwell on it.

Were the Kaiaphons somehow responsible for the disappearance of the child Chillos, and the insurrectionist Thestas? How else could she interpret it? Why would the passageway, underneath the city, lead directly to the dungeon of City Prison, and the cell where the two were held?

The doors of the House of Assembly were open, and the bells, ringing in the tower, announced that a meeting was in session.

Demiarchs in chitons and blue sashes were hurrying from all corners of the city.

The House of Assembly, bordering City Square, was the seat of Thénai's government, the heart of its democracy, the center of its politics. How many countless times had Khloë entered these sacred halls, these revered chambers? And now she returned with a new attitude, one of abject distrust, not just of Dioscouro and his administration but distrust of every demiarch, every whispered word, every hidden intention. There were Old Believers in this city. Old Believers! She had not left behind the troubles of Bastos; they had re-emerged here, in this city, among her friends and fellow travelers, in the highest seats of government.

~

Dioscouro stood in the center of the House of Assembly's meeting hall, surrounded at all sides by hundreds of demiarchs, seated on benches. Khloë took her place in the shadows, away from the prying eyes. She intended to only be an observer.

Though she had lost much trust in Dioscouro, he seemed to never want her out of her sight. Perhaps, the strength and courage of an amazon reassured him. Or perhaps, she knew too much, about the nature of what had been placed in Amara's temple, about the anger and dissent of the tributary cities, about how he had tolerated Old Believers all for the sake of silver and gold.

"Friends, Thenoans, citizens," Dioscouro began, "believers in freedom, in liberty and in democracy, I have called this meeting for the sake of our great and glorious league, for the sake of our cause, which shines, brighter than ever before."

"Get on with it!" a demiarch shouted, and a few chuckles echoed throughout the hall.

"I know some of you were worried after Floridion and Bregantion withdrew from the League," Dioscouro said, "but we have found ways of replacing their tribute. The treasury at Choros overflows, and there is no end to our funds. The future of the League remains secure."

Khloë had not realized Floridion and Bregantion withdrew entirely; the fight, which started on the High City, must have been much more intense than she'd thought.

"How is that possible?" one of the demiarchs shouted. "Bregantion gave us three *talents* every month!"

"Our citizens have stepped up their contributions," Dioscouro said. "Do not worry yourselves! We are on the very cusp of winning this war. The very cusp!"

How many times had that been said before?

As the meeting drew on, spilling over into the obscure minutiae of Thénai's budget, Khloë noted a woman standing in the shadows, dressed in scarlet, with a gold-and-diamond brooch over her neck. Her fingers were studded with rings of sapphire, ruby and emerald. Her gown was cinched with a gold belt. She was quietly watching, quietly observing as the deliberations continued.

Khloë had never seen the woman before, but clearly she was a woman of some import. Not just anyone was allowed to watch the House of Assembly's proceedings.

Eventually, the Assembly meeting ended with a prayer for the prosperity and success of the League; then Dioscouro announced its adjournment.

The demiarchs began to filter out, going home, whether it was to the seaside villas of the Harbor District or the urban townhomes outside City Square. Yet the scarlet woman remained. Her eyes at last met Khloë's, and Khloë quickly looked away. Hers was an intense gaze, one you couldn't hold for long.

Eventually, the only ones who remained in the meeting hall were Khloë, Dioscouro and the scarlet woman.

"Ah! Elena! I did not see you!" Dioscouro said as he walked over to her. He laid hold of her gingerly, and pecked each cheek. "It has been a while."

"A week is not too long, my sweet," she said. "And who is this lovely young woman?"

Elena was flattering her. Khloë was by no means young, and she was not a woman but an amazon. She bowed her head. "Hello."

"Khloë, senior advisor," Dioscouro said and motioned to her, "meet Elena Kaiaphon, patriot and financier of the war effort. We could not have retaken Thénai without her or her family."

Khloë's stomach dropped and a lump had formed in her throat, one she could not shake. All she could think of, when she peered into Elena Kaiaphon's eyes, was Chillos, missing from his cell.

"My dear Dioscouro," Elena Kaiaphon said, "tomorrow

night, you are invited to a grand feast at the nymphaeum in House Kaiaphon. We are honoring patriotism and this, our war, our glorious revolution. You are invited as well, my dear amazon. There shall be delicious wines and foods served. We only ask that every attendee bring her best clothes, and some sort of offering to our cause, the Thenoan League."

Khloë did not want to venture into that dark place. Who knew what secrets the House Kaiaphon held? But for the sake of Chillos, and only for the sake of Chillos, she would enter it.

BOS, BORDER OF KERSICA AND THENOA

For days, the garrison at Bos had held against Axander's assault. But the gate had crumbled, and each hour, more hoplites had perished. Eventually, the resistance began to crumble, giving way to a rout, and panic overtook the ranks.

Taicho fought as hard as he could, swinging spear and shield, but the best he could do was defend himself. As a green recruit, his skills were vastly limited compared to the Kersican hoplites, and in all these days and hours of fighting, he had not taken a single life.

Nestor, shouting wildly, demanded they abandon the battlements. Ladders continued to pour down, but in the center of the fortress was high ground, a keep, where the Free and Democratic Armies would make their last stand. He and Pythio fled down the steps, away from the wall, as the chaos spread. Kersicans began pouring over the walls, slaying those who didn't flee fast enough.

Breathlessly, Taicho ran alongside the inner walls of the fortress, bolting away, beside stables and armories, until at last he reached the gate. He sprinted inside the keep just as gate slammed shut, leaving Free and Democratic soldiers to be slaughtered like pigs.

Pythio was by Taicho's side, panting heavily.

Taicho, malnourished and dehydrated, wanted nothing more than his waterskin.

In all these days, Pythio had said not a word, save for prayers muttered under his breath.

Taicho keeled over and tried to breathe. At last he removed his helm and let it fall from his hands. For the first time in days, the wind rustled through his hair, which was wet with sweat. The sun was bright and glaring, but after fighting for so long in such poor conditions, it felt like the crispness of spring. The air had never smelled sweeter, and the weight on his shoulders had been lifted.

He dropped his shield and spear and stretched his arms.

"Taicho!" The voice of Nestor echoed from far away. "At attention!"

But he was too exhausted to wear his helm, too fatigued to bear his weapons. He'd had enough. If he did not relax, if he did not refresh himself, he would die.

He reached for his waterskin, but he knew it was empty. Still, he unclipped it from his belt, wrung it near his lips, and confirmed it was dry. At last, he cast it onto the dusty ground and muttered curses.

Taicho sank to his knees.

But Pythio's shadow fell over him. "Here," Pythio said. "Drink."

Taicho looked up at him.

Pythio was offering him his waterskin.

"Thank the gods for you," Taicho mumbled.

He took the half-full waterskin and squeezed the last bits of ice-cold moisture into his mouth.

He drank every drop of it, but when Taicho stood up, he was still exhausted, still dehydrated. "Thank you," he said again, and handed Pythio the waterskin.

He took it and slinked off like a shadow amid the gloom.

Taicho knew he had no choice but to don his armor once more. He laid the too-heavy helm upon his head, picked up his spear and shield, and headed away, toward the battlements, toward the inner walls of Bos' keep.

Above the gate, Taicho stood, his shield locked in formation. Pythio was by his side.

Below them, the Kersicans had gathered.

Out of the ranks, Axander emerged, a sword in his left hand and a sling in his right. He was not dressed for war, but there was not a wound on him. Over the days of battle, he had always fought at the front, together with his troops. Despite being Taicho's mortal enemy, Taicho had gained some grudging respect for Axander… respect mixed with terror, for it would surely be his army that ended all their lives.

"A last offer!" Axander shouted. "A final proposal, Nestor! We mean no harm to the Thenoan League, none whatsoever! We are hunters seeking a bounty… hunters of a powerful creature."

Taicho wondered if there was any truth to his words.

"Let us pass by," Axander said, "and we shall spare all your lives."

Over the silence of the day, the voice of Nestor echoed: "You Kersicans may view the Free and Democratic Armies as limp and weak, but we are not! We are honorable, and we fight to the end. For Bos, for Thénai, for the League… for liberty and for democracy all around the sea… all around the world!"

At his words, the Free and Democratic soldiers began to shout. Nestor had stoked a fire within them, a fire which had waned over these long days of battle. Now, rejuvenated, full of purpose, Taicho lifted his spear into the air and braced his shield against his chest. He would not die in vain. Perhaps, he would not be remembered; but it was for liberty's sake he would perish, for the freedom of Lornadion and every colony throughout the world.

"You have made your choice!" Axander said. "But it is a foolish one. We are not fighting the Thenoan League… we are mere hunters. So be it! I will be glad to take you to your graves!"

Here they would fight; here they would make their last

stand. There was no better commander than Nestor Kaiaphon to fight with, no better leader to face danger and death alongside. Here Taicho would perish… for Thénai's sake, and for Lornadion's.

~

The battle began immediately… ladders falling on the walls, shouting, screaming, the glint of swords and sabers, and utter chaos. The sun burned hot upon Taicho's helm, and his thirst returned immediately, ravening, ravishing, destructive. Nestor's words no longer comforted him.

I will die. I will be forgotten. Not even Mother and Father will remember me…

As the sun began to set in the west, glowing with orange and red fire, Axander and his men breached the walls. One by one, the Kersican hoplites began to fall.

Pythio fled, and something about the sight of the young man fleeing vanquished whatever courage Taicho had.

Taicho turned and fled in pursuit, breaking the formation, opening up weakness in the shield wall. Loud cries of death rang out as Taicho followed Pythio in a mad pursuit.

It was by Pythio's hand that the army broke rank. It was by Pythio, and by Taicho's hand, that the Kersicans claimed victory.

~

In the central yard of the keep, Pythio had discarded his helm, revealing his closely-cropped black hair, his swarthy face, burned by the sun. Taicho had joined him; and now Taicho was a coward, too.

The Eloesian tradition said a hoplite must return bearing his shield, or dead, upon a bier.

Taicho could not live as a coward back home. Even in Lornadion, he'd be exiled. His father would be ashamed of him; his mother would not speak of him.

As Axander's troops poured over the walls, Pythio fell to his knees and raised his hands in surrender.

Taicho cast his helm aside, then threw down his spear and shield. Then he, too, fell to his knees and raised his hands. They had taken the coward's way out; now, as cowards, they would die.

The Kersicans, in their red capes and red-crested helms, began to fill the courtyard. Bearing spears and shields, they nonetheless let Pythio and Taicho alone, kneeling there, in pathetic surrender.

As the Free and Democratic soldiers began to fall, they plunged headlong from the battlements. Taicho and Pythio had broken the shield formation, creating an insurmountable weakness.

The blood of Nestor Kaiaphon, and all the hoplites who served them, were on their hands.

But the battle had been lost long before Pythio fled in cowardice. There was no way they could hold them off forever. They had been days, perhaps just hours, from final vanquishment.

But that knowledge did not help Taicho's guilt. He could not help what his father would think, what his grandfather would think—his grandfather, a veteran of many wars. As a shade, floating in the River of Souls, did the actions of his cowardly son reach his ears? Was that added to his punishment in the underworld? What was worse, his gloomy existence, or the fact that he had helped bring Taicho into the world?

The screams began to die down, and the more silent the evening became, the more Kersicans began to fill the yard.

Through the crowd, Taicho made out many bodies,

twitching in the heat of the day.

Nestor Kaiaphon was dead. All his hoplites were dead. Everyone Taicho had gotten to know and fought alongside were dead. Pythio and Taicho alone were responsible; at least, that was how it seemed.

The Kersicans filled the yard, a mosaic of red capes and bronze breastplates. Out of the homogeneity, Axander emerged, dressed like none of the others, un-armored, a headband puffing up his brown hair, a sword in his left hand, a sling in his right.

He was smiling. "Cowards! And so young," he said. "It is always a pity to spill young blood."

Would he kill them? Taicho wondered. They surely deserved it.

"What are your names?" Axander said. "Speak, or I will reconsider my mercy."

"Pythio!"

"Taicho!"

He had never heard Pythio speak so loud.

"Pythio and Taicho, Free and Democratic Soldiers… I am your enemy," Axander said, "but you are fortunate. Your enemy is merciful, full of grace. You are worth more to me dead than alive. Eloesians would never buy an Eloesian slave; but a southron would jump at the chance. I could get many *thalon* for you.

"And that will be your fate if you do not stay with us. Stay silent and obedient, and we will let you live.

"I did not lie to your foolish commander; we are not the enemies of the Thenoan League. We are hunting a beast from another world… he drank the Stygian water and he changed."

Memories returned of lessons, taught in Lornadion's town square. In ancient times, a being from heaven had fallen into a vast lake; his power had filled the water, suffusing it with energy. In that water, the great hero Phillipidēs had dipped his newly-forged sword.

But those were ancient times, and Stygian water was a myth. At least, that was what Taicho had thought.

"You will help us kill him," Axander said. "You will slay the monster with us, or you will perish with us."

Taicho had heard of Stygian blades, and Stygian shields; but *drinking* Stygian water? What would happen if someone did that?

HIDDEN POND, OUTSIDE ARCTOS, ISTEROI KINGDOM

It was late one evening, and the heat of the day had hardly dwindled, when the white bird returned to Geon.

The light of Geon's halo, the glow of his wings, reflected on the white bird's reddish eyes.

It looked at him this way, then that.

For Geon, hearing the tongue of beasts had been difficult to get used to. But now he could speak to the animals of the earth, and they could hear him; moreover, they were drawn to him, and revered him as a master and a lord.

"Have you found Herodota?" Geon asked the white bird.

The bird darted over and perched on one on his fingers.

"My lord, I was flying through the place near the river, where the fish are and where the great wooden fish float in…"

It clearly meant the harbor.

"I was searching through the homes there, and I saw one had its lattice window open… and there, I could hear a woman singing, as beautiful as any bird…she was singing a hymn, and halfway through, she began to weep and speak of Amara. Then she shut her window, and I saw no more."

That was Herodota; he was sure of it.

If only he had some bread to feed the bird, some sort of treat to offer it. Instead, his only offering would be thanks.

"Thank you, white bird," Geon muttered. "Thank you, thank you."

"It is my pleasure," the white bird said without moving its beak.

It did not fly away; instead it basked in Geon's light and warmth, not wanting to leave.

It seemed that those who drew near Geon, and embraced him, never departed his presence without urging. It was not just light he radiated; he radiated something else, something immaterial, something inexplicable.

As the bird kept its talons around Geon's fingers, its memories seemed to flood into Geon's mind.

He saw the priestess in her home on the river's shore, the window formed of iron grills and glass. She was on an upper story, and tears were in her eyes. She had shaved her head, like all priestesses of Amara did; but now she was overcome with emotion.

She retreated into a closet and a while later, emerged in the blue gown of a priestess. She laid over her head a black wig, the same ones priestesses wore. Then she fell to her knees, lifted her hands to the heavens, and began to weep, and to pray.

~

She was petitioning Amara. "Help! Help!" she said. "Help us, mother of all! I have seen the horror in the sanctuary... and I have seen what is coming! Stop what is coming, Amara! Stop it, for the sake of Thénai, which once loved you!"

HIGH CITY, THÉNAI

The cool of the morning greeted Khloë as she stepped out of the House of the Archon.

Dread hung over her like a baleful sword; she knew full well that the Kaiaphons' party was set for today.

And moreover, she knew that somehow, some way, the Kaiaphons had a hand in the disappearance of Chillos and the insurrectionist Thestas, that the passageway that wound its way to City Prison had ended at their very door.

Khloë would do her best to find him. In some spare moment, at some late hour, she would wander off from the party and search, as well as she could, for Chillos. His parents deserved nothing less.

~

Dressed in a gown of blue silk, with her hair tied in a long braid, Khloë followed Dioscouro and a few other high officials out of the High City, down a ramp into the streets below.

As they made their way, flanked by bodyguards, through Thénai, it was more evident than ever that life had returned.

The streets were as full as they had been in the city's height, overrun with horses and merchants and women passing to-and-fro. Yet Thénai's return to glory could not ease the feeling in Khloë's gut. Her stomach twisted to knots.

It seemed she, alone, knew who the Kaiaphons truly were; it seemed she, alone, wished to expunge Old Believers from Thénai's ranks. Perhaps Dioscouro knew; perhaps he was aware of what was going on.

But the poor in the city of Thénai were more pious than the rich; having nothing, many clung to the gods and the promise of eternal reward. If they discovered what Dioscouro had tolerated, riots would erupt, and violence would engulf the city and its environs.

Why had the Kaiaphons agreed to continue their financing of the Thenoan cause, even now, now that the statue of their damnable god had been removed? Why, Khloë wondered? Perhaps, she would know soon.

~

The gates of the House Kaiaphon were open. Guards stood at either end, guards dressed in the manner of hoplites, with bronze breastplates and white horsehair crests on their helmets.

In the courtyard of the House Kaiaphon, flanked by porticoes, Elena stood, garbed in the same scarlet gown as before. Her hair had been tied in a bun, and the jeweled rings of her fingers gleamed in the sun.

"Welcome!" she cried, smiling, and rushed over to Dioscouro, then kissed him on his cheeks. "Ah, amazon, I am so very glad you could make it. I dare predict you shall enjoy yourself, very much."

"Ah, Theon!" she said to another. "Ah! Megala! Ah! Neimora!"

She greeted each member of Thénai's government with her overwrought, and, Khloë guessed, false, excitement. As a rich woman, a member of Thénai's most prestigious social circles, perhaps putting on a facade was necessary, but in truth it disgusted Khloë.

In the amazon world, pleasantries were avoided; and the silver tongue of a social climber was regarded with disgust.

Sometimes, Khloë really did miss home. Perhaps, the amazon world was where she belonged.

Elena Kaiaphon led the party through the mansion, making comment on its various treasures and displays.

"Here," she said, pointing to a silver necklace studded with an emerald, "is the very necklace which Sosimon wore during the Megaran War! I purchased it from a trader in Tharta, years ago! It cost only seventy-five *doukon*."

"Only" seventy-five *doukon*. Khloë did her best to hide her disgust. Such a price could pay a laborer's salary for many months. She was not surprised how out-of-touch Elena Kaiaphon was, or what a braggart she had been, but it still grated on her.

"Here," Elena said, and pointed to a pair of bronze figurines in a display case, "these 'little gods' are from Khazidea."

Behind the glass case, against a backdrop of red cloth, the tiny creatures lay. The bronze had a greenish tint. They appeared men from the bottom down, but their heads were those of crocodiles.

Khloë had been to that blasted land, in the presence of Theron, though no crocodile had ever taken her. The monstrous creatures often lay in wait at the bottom of the Khazan River, eyes open, ready to pounce if a prey drew near.

"My grandfather purchased them from an artificer last century," Elena said. "They were my playthings when I was a little girl."

The "little gods" were finely made, with minute detail on their faces and bodies, but they were a pitiful excuse for a child's plaything.

"And here! Here is my most treasured possession." At the end of the hall, Elena motioned to a gold sarcophagus, forged with human features. "This is the resting place of a great Khazidean king… It is priceless. My grandfather also purchased this. He said it was by legal means, but I suspect he bought it from tomb raiders."

"Tomb raiders!" Dioscouro exclaimed.

"Yes, the great king Magon the First, King of the Two Khazideas, from the sea to the desert, from the shore to the shore." Elena's pride was palpable.

Though no doubt Magon's memory had faded, and his reign was a scribbled note in the history books, he wondered what his descendants would think if they found out. Their ancestor, so many generations removed from them, was not resting in his chosen burial place, but in the home of Elena Kaiaphon, a foreigner, an exploiter of the Thenoan people, an Old Believer.

As they turned down more corridors, Khloë noted the presence of many doors, some locked, some open. Finding Chillos in such a place would be a difficult proposition. Perhaps, it would be impossible. But Khloë would try as best she could. She did not care what the Kaiaphons thought. If she was discovered, and Dioscouro exiled her from Thénai, so be it. She would leave the human world with her head held high. She would return to Amazonia, the place of her birth, having tried to correct a great wrong.

"Chillos," she found herself muttering under her breath, "where are you? Let me find you… Cry out, as loud as you can…"

Eventually, the tour through Elena's vanity ended at a gold-lined door.

"Here," Elena said. "A surprise. I promise you shall not be disappointed. In, through this door, is our nymphaeum.

"To get to the party, you must all be in your underclothes."

Dioscouro gasped. A few of the women who accompanied them began to blush.

"Are you sure?" Dioscouro protested lightly, but Khloë knew that whatever Elena Kaiaphon wanted, she got.

Except, of course, the statue in the Temple of Amara, now removed from its place.

One by one, Elena's guests began to oblige.

Khloë was the last to obey, removing her gown, down to the small shift that served as her underclothes.

The semi-clothed Elena then opened the door. Music flooded out from within. They had come to the nymphaeum.

~

White columns surrounded a vast pool. Up above, the sun was shining; there was no roof.

Near the edge of the pool, a group of musicians were playing instruments: lyres, drums, cymbals and harps in a cascading melody.

In the waters of the pool, platters were floating like lilies, offering all manners of food: on one sausages, on another strips of pork, on yet another sweetcakes drizzled with honey. Bottles of wine also floated, and saucers for drinking.

The servants in this "nymphaeum" were dressed like their namesake, like nymphs, with horns on their heads and white gowns covering their bodies. On their feet were sandals made to look like hooves.

Elena Kaiaphon had spared no expense or flourish to impress, and for once on this baleful journey, Khloë smiled. Elena Kaiaphon had done cruel things, abominable things, and Chillos remained on Khloë's mind above all else; but Elena was determined for her guests to have a grand time.

The water was cool, and refreshing as it covered Khloë's body, but as soon as the partygoers joined her, the familiar dread returned, the worry, the knowledge of what she meant to do. Khloë intended to find Chillos, one way or another, and bring him back to his family—dead or alive. Perhaps, then, Dioscouro would break his ties with these wicked people. No money was worth having an Old Believer in the League's ranks.

Dioscouro was an old man; he was no gazelle leaping from this place to that, but he swam through the waters of the pool with the speed and litheness of an athlete. "Ah! Elena! You have outdone yourself," he said. "I have been to many parties in many nymphaeums; but this is certainly the best. Surely, Seladora, queen of the nymphs, is envious of you."

"Ah… I doubt it," Elena said. She picked up a sweetcake from one of the floating platters and began to nibble at it. "Seladora is enthroned in heaven, with the nymphs at her side. This, my dear Dioscouro, is mere imitation."

Piety she exuded, or tried to; but Khloë knew her heart, her intentions. The Old Believers did not regard the pantheon with anything approaching respect. To them, Seladora and all the other gods were nothing more than jests; or, at best, mortal foes they only grudgingly respected. This nymphaeum, made to look like a holy grotto, sacred to nymphs, was only a means to impress their neighbors.

The whole party struck Khloë as inappropriate, in a time of such trouble city-wide, when refugees went hungry and returned to destroyed homes; but she knew Dioscouro's intent. The Kaiaphons had such fabulous wealth that they formed a great portion of the war's budget. To reject Elena's display of ostentation would be the height of folly.

But all Khloë could think of, amid this sumptuous banquet, half-submerged in the cold waters of the nymphaeum, was Chillos. She did not know what the boy looked like, but she knew his parents were poor; and his life was as valuable, or more, than any of the Kaiaphons, rich and important though they might be.

She wondered what Elena's intention was in inviting them here, to this splendid and decadent party. She had seen the human heart, in all its workings, and knew there was a hidden purpose behind each action, one that was often kept hidden. No doubt she had invited Khloë as an afterthought; but that little mistake would be her downfall. She would find Chillos, abducted from his prison cell, and then, the whole city would know of the Kaiaphons' dark hearts.

"Tell me," Elena said, half-swimming, half-wading.

She was looking at Khloë, and Khloë shuddered.

"You are an amazon," she said. "Do the amazons swear allegiance to the Kersican or Thenoan Leagues?"

Khloë tried not to glare. "Amazons are concerned with their own lives. Their own lands. Their own islands. With survival. Food. Water. Drink. Only amazons who have moved mainland have any concerns with this war. You will find I am the exception."

It was clear Elena did not favor her response; she had pursed her lips and wrinkled her brow.

It was true; in the wider human world, it seemed each tribe and nation had picked a side.

But to Amazonia, it was a petty concern; and whether the Kersican League won, or the Thenoan League seized the victory, or the gods returned to earth, amazons did not much care. Humanity was not their concern; only their own homes and farms, their own islands, their own families and their own children had any bearing on their lives. They had lost the Amazon-Eloesian War; and now, as Amazonia faded in power and relevance, their connection to the wider world had begun to taper away.

"I thought the whole world had picked a side," Elena said dismissively.

The amazons had intervened in the Southron War; but a fight between brothers in Eloesus was of no concern to them. One tribe of Eloesians was practically indistinguishable from the other.

And as Khloë stood there in the water, with no appetite, gazing upon the sumptuous feast, floating like lilies in the pool, she wondered once more whether Amazonia was where she belonged.

Certainly, she was a fish out of water; she did not truly belong anywhere except Amazonia. She had received Thenoan citizenship; she had made offerings to the civic gods, and her name was registered in the temple. According to the law, she was a member of the Eloesian nation, a Thenoan in every way; but she never would truly belong.

From one of the lily-like platters, Elena grabbed a bottle of wine, uncorked it, and began to pour it into saucers. "Cheers, my friends, to patriotism."

Wading through the water, she pushed the saucers to each member of the party. The music, played on the lyre and drum, seemed to reach a cascading crescendo.

"To my brother, Nestor, who is—even now—defending our city and our glorious cause," Elena said. "To Bos and all those fighting under beloved Nestor; may its walls stand firm, and all who fight against it falter."

Everyone took a sip, except Khloe. She could not bear to honor a Kaiaphon, not even a brave veteran, fighting in a far-off fortress at great risk to his life.

"I'm sorry," Khloë said. "I've come down with something. I must… I must…"

"The lavatory is not far," Elena said. "Taddaeos…"

One of the servants, a swarthy southron, approached. "My lady." He took a bow.

Khloë ascended the pool stairs. She did not know how she would escape Taddaeos' watchful eye, but she would search the Kaiaphons' residence, every inch of it.

~

Taddaeos led her down the marble corridors, beside busts of great thinkers and gold-framed pictures of Themurian hills and mountains. There were so many doors, so many chambers, that doubt had begun to grow in Khloë's mind, nagging and persistent doubt. But what was doubt compared to the thought of Chillos, a poor boy from Potters' Street, taken from his family in a great injustice, and then kidnapped by these wicked people? If the Kaiaphons had not gotten to him first, Khloë would find him and rescue him; or else, she would perish in the attempt.

At last, Taddaeos opened a door, and outside, in the air, was a toilet enclosed by a wooden fence.

"Here you go, my lady," Taddaeos said.

As a warrior in the amazon army, Khloë had been taught not only the art of the sword, glaive and chakram, but also the best techniques of hand-to-hand combat.

With a firm strike of the hand, puncturing Taddaeos' neck, she sent the servant to his knees, and then face-first onto the floor, completely unconscious. She would have a few minutes, at least, to explore the Kaiaphons' mansion unmolested.

Surely, she looked like a madwoman, wearing nothing more than her shirt, dripping wet, leaving a trail of water wherever she walked. But it did not matter; nothing mattered besides Chillos, the poor boy she swore to save.

She had witnessed what the Old Believers did; where the New Gods demanded cattle as a blood offering, the ancient gods demanded human blood, and the blood of the young delighted them most. She had witnessed it in none other than Bastos, a haunt of Old Believers half a world away. She had never thought such evil existed within Thénai's walls, but over these weeks and months, she had begun to question everything and everyone. It seemed every person she once knew wore a mask: Dioscouro, Phalco, the Kaiaphons. How could she trust anyone again?

~

Through the Kaiaphons' mansion Khloë ran, through vestibules painted in vivid colors, through halls lined with mirrors, beside displays of ancient artifacts and corridors lined with statues

There was a library, full of scrolls and books; there was a study full of ledgers and papers. There were larders full of various spices and grains. There were multiple dining rooms, with chairs and tables of teak and oak. But the more she hurried along, the more she peered through each door, both opened and closed, the more it dawned on her that she was alone. Chillos was nowhere to be found.

At last, she reached the foyer of the Kaiaphons' mansion, where she had entered, and there was a great commotion in the distance. Elena Kaiaphon had been alerted.

But amid the marble floors, Khloë noted a loose tile with what looked like a handle. As the sound of footsteps echoed, and the hysterical shouts of Elena, Khloë seized upon the handle and jerked it open.

A ladder led downwards into the dark.

Khloë quickly descended, into the musty air, into the gloom.

~

Underneath the House of Kaiaphon was a vast cellar. The floor was of dirt, and all around, on its side and on its middle, there were stone sarcophagi in the manner of Khazidean kings: the faces of dead Kaiaphons etched into the stone, depicted with sunray crowns on their heads.

"Chillos!" Khloë began to cry in desperation. "Chillos!"

But all that greeted her was silence, here, in the House of Kaiaphon, here, in the house of the dead.

"What is the meaning of this?" Elena howled from up

above.

Taddaeos and a number of other servants had begun to descend.

"You are under arrest, Khloë!" Dioscouro roared from a distance. "Your madness has gone far enough!"

Taddaeos seized Khloë's arm, and another servant seized her neck.

Khloë did not resist.

She had done her best to find Chillos. She had failed. She had failed him, and she had failed herself.

Now, punishment awaited her. Despite herself, she began to weep. She wept for Thénai, she wept for herself, she wept for Amazonia. But most of all, she wept for Chillos, and for the victims of Old Believers all across the world.

OUTSIDE BOS, THENOA

Pythio and Taicho, the only survivors of Nestor Kaiaphon's regiment, followed Axander, for there was nowhere else to go.

For some reason, Axander had spared them.

Taicho's cowardice had saved his life; but at what cost?

Perhaps, in the end, this would not work out well for him.

As the afternoon cast long shadows over the shrubs and plane trees, all Taicho could think of, as he marched, were those he had left behind.

Countless hundreds of Free and Democratic soldiers had perished in the Battle of Bos. But it was Nestor Kaiaphon, the commander, that Taicho thought of most. He was a brave man, an inspiration to all hoplites that fought under him, and Taicho had gained undying respect for him; but under his firm words and commanding presence, Taicho sensed a gloom, a darkness he hid from all those around him. Even when he smiled, there was little light in his eyes.

But he had fallen; and when Pythio broke rank, Taicho had followed. The shield wall had been disrupted, leaving the hoplites of Nestor's regiment open for the slaughter.

Whose fault was it, ultimately? Pythio's. But Taicho had followed him. He had not perished. He had not achieved the beautiful death that warrior poets wrote about.

He had never wanted a beautiful death. The concept was alien to him. There was nothing beautiful about death; not even perishing as a hero. All would eventually descend to the underworld, and float through the River of Souls as gloomy shades. How could you ever celebrate that, even if you were remembered among the living? As a shade, you knew nothing, floating about, despairing and pondering.

"That's enough!" Axander lifted his hand. "Enough for one day. We rest here."

In the distance, there was a small spring, ringed with stones.

Far in the distance, sheep grazed on a hill, white tufts against the green. They were far from civilization, far from cities.

When Taicho reached Thénai, he had marveled at the size and at the grandeur of the buildings. This countryside of hills and shepherds' flocks reminded him of home. Lornadion was far away and yet dear to his heart: but could he ever return as a coward? His father would disown him. His mother would be ashamed.

"Gather firewood!" Axander shouted to his men who, despite the taxing battle, still numbered in the thousands.

Ballistae and catapults also had survived intact. But whatever they hunted, whether it were an elephant or even a hydra, such immense weapons seemed too much.

Taicho and Pythio were still bound, completely disarmed, wearing nothing more than their tunics and breeches. They were utterly at Axander's mercy.

Perhaps, Axander thought he could sell Taicho for a ransom; but who would pay? His parents were not wealthy by any means. And what worth was a coward to the city of Thénai?

As the afternoon faded into evening, and the grass was cast in red and gold, Taicho and Pythio sat down. The heat was fading. In the distance, soldiers were gathering bucketfuls of water from the spring. Others were gathering sticks and kindling for the fire. In the gloom, Pythio and Taicho were alone.

It was a wonder that, in all this time, Pythio had remained distant from Taicho, not saying a word. Even in captivity, he was a mystery; he was as cold and remote as ever.

As for speaking to him, as for inquiring, Taicho had learned not to try. He would never learn who this Pythio was, this Pythio, who had turned and ran, who had broken formation, and hastened the inevitable slaughter of the Free and Democratic soldiers.

Taicho had followed him in his reckless flight. He had spared Taicho's life at great cost to his honor.

Would Pythio's parents reject him as a coward? Taicho would never know.

~

Axander's hoplites crafted a bonfire of logs and branches, and overlaid it with kindling. As night fell and the moon arose, Axander struck a flint and tinder, and the bonfire erupted into flame.

Axander's hoplites talked amongst themselves. They had removed their breastplates and helmets.

As the night deepened, Axander approached. He swept aside his headband, letting his brown hair fall free.

"My lord," said one of the hoplites, "how far off to our prey?"

These mercenaries were interested in gold. Taicho wondered how much Axander had promised them.

There was a commotion to Taicho's left: the sound of crunching twigs and grass.

The flickering light of the campfire reflected on three forms.

There were two women walking toward them, garbed in blue hoods. One held a sword of wood, another a book.

But what walked between them frightened Taicho most.

The hulking brute of a creature, half again as tall as the women, had the appearance of a bull, with horns and twinkling golden eyes. Yet he walked upright, with his cloven feet grinding the grass beneath them. A gold ring was in his snout, and strapped to his back was a great axe of iron.

Taicho found himself creeping backward.

What was this creature? He felt like he had seen something like it before, perhaps in a painting or in some fresco.

If the creature frightened Axander, he showed no sign of it.

Axander did not so much as draw his sword.

"My lord Axander." The woman with the book curtsied.

"My lady Euridikē," answered Axander. He bowed slightly. "You have come to bring news, I hope."

"I would not waste your time," Euridikē answered. "Have I ever disappointed you before?"

Axander was looking at the brutish creature.

"Do not fear Lord Skauros," Euridikē said. "He is a servant, like you; an agent of the Oracle's work. He harms only her enemies."

Axander bowed again, but the bull-like creature only grunted.

"The monster you hunt was seen near Arctos," Euridikē said. "In the land of the Isteroi."

"He is hiding among barbarians!" Axander said. "A fitting place for him."

Euridikē smiled. "The King of the Isteroi has agreed to help our cause. But only a hero, such as yourself, will be able to slay Geon."

Geon? A monster named Geon? Taicho laughed at the thought. In Lornadion, villagers had given common names to dogs and cats, but none as familiar and provincial as Geon.

"He has retreated outside of Arctos," Euridikē said. "He tried to enter the city twice. But he turned back. He refused to hurt the guards.

"I do not know why he wishes to enter the city. Neither does sacred Io."

"The Oracle herself does not know something." Axander balked. "It is hard to believe."

"And yet," Euridikē said. "You were called to serve her. This, my dear Axander, is your sacred task. Go north, to the Isteroi Kingdom. The monster you hunt is outside the city walls. You will find him there."

HIDDEN POND, OUTSIDE ARCTOS, ISTEROI KINGDOM

The night had fallen, and the stars were shining brighter than Geon had ever remembered. The moon was white and full. Some wispy clouds veiled it, like a cloak, and despite the stillness of the air, and the solitude of the night, Geon had a bad feeling, one he couldn't quite shake. A feeling of dread hung over him. *Something will happen tonight*, a voice told him. *Something consequential.*

The forest animals had not emerged to greet him, an unusual event for certain.

Normally, in the evening, he would bathe, but he remained clothed, with the Spear and Shield of Pegara at the ready. He did not know what was coming, but he would remain alert and prepared for whatever the night had in store for him.

Eventually, he found himself walking away, through the veil of trees, and eventually, to the wheat fields.

Below, the lights of the City of Arctos gleamed.

And amid the pale light of the moon, dark shapes were moving, a crowd hundreds strong.

Though he was too far away to see much of anything, he sensed the presence of Andar, the man who had come to hunt him and then left to find Herodota.

But against the moonlight, he noted the gleam of metal: swords and daggers, knives and pitchforks. They had not come for peaceful purposes.

Now, Geon knew; Andar had returned home, to Arctos, and the peace and light of Geon's presence had faded. Perhaps, his wife had scolded him. A great price was on Geon's head; a price that could make anyone rich. What do you mean, his wife had said, that you refused to kill him?

As Geon expected, Andar was at the head of the party, but his face was hidden in a helmet, and now he was well prepared, with a breastplate, a buckler and a sword. Beside him, numbering two-hundred, were an assortment of Arctos commoners bearing common implements, and at the front, members of the royal guard with blue plumes on their helmets.

Andar had led this group of miscreants straight to Geon.

In the end, it was the white bird who had helped Geon, who had told him, in truth, where Herodota, priestess of Amara, had hidden herself. It was Andar who had betrayed him unto death. But it would not end well for him. It would not end well for anyone gathered here.

"There he is!" The voice of Andar carried above the shuffling of feet, above the cooing of the night birds and the chirping of the crickets. "The monster! I told you he was here!"

"Andar!" Geon answered, and though he did not shout, his voice resounded over the hills. His wings began to luminesce, to shine white, like the sun. The glowing of his body reflected in the eyes of the crowd, and some of them began to falter and fall back.

"You have betrayed me, Andar!" Geon said. "Why have you betrayed me?"

There were tears in Andar's eyes; though Geon could not see them, he could sense them.

"Be warned!" Geon continue. "If you draw any closer, I will defend myself! If you value your life, do not approach me."

For a while, it seemed they obeyed. They remained frozen in place, some in fear, some in regret or trepidation.

But with a shout, Andar charged, heaving his sword behind

his back and his buckler high.

The King of Isteros himself had awarded Andar those weapons. But those weapons would be Andar's downfall.

Andar swung his blade at Geon, and Geon parried with the Shield of Pegara.

Andar's sword shattered in two, and the smoldering brand fell to the ground, giving off smoke.

Geon smote him, and Andar went flying, hurtling through the fields.

Others came charging, and Geon parried, striking when necessary. Eventually they turned and fled, sprinting through the hills, toward the lights of the City of Arctos.

One warrior lay maimed, twitching, on the ground, as he bled out on the grass.

In the distance, Andar was howling in pain, clutching his side. No doubt, many bones had been broken. If something was not done, Andar would die as a crippled beggar in the city; his wife would leave him, taking their children with her. He would be buried in an unmarked grave, forgotten for all time.

The warrior, twitching, in the spasms of death, would die soon anyway; for he was not near as healthy as he seemed.

Still, Geon walked over to him, stooped down, and stretched out his hand. White fire hovered above his fingers as the wounds began to seal, and strength returned to the warrior's body. Eventually, he gasped, and his eyes opened wide. He let out a scream and scrambled to his feet, then sprinted away, toward the city gate.

Geon followed the sound of Andar's groaning.

As Geon looked upon him, anger rose up within him, anger he couldn't quench.

Geon had spared Andar's life once. Why should he make the same mistake? He did not deserve a second chance.

He deserved the future that was in store for him; living as a crippled, hungry beggar on the streets of Arctos, until the plague took him.

There was no excuse for his greed. He considered money more important than the sacred mission Geon had sent him on. Moreover, he had turned back, with murder in his eyes. He had been intent on taking Geon's life, the life of the one who had spared him.

"Mercy," he was mumbling. "Mercy… mercy, please."

Geon placed the head of the Spear of Pegara on Andar's throat. A little pressure, a small thrust, and Geon could end everything for Andar. But he hesitated. He stopped himself.

"Andar," Geon said. "I will spare you once again. But you must do as you said before. Herodota lives in the harbor, in a house with lattice windows."

"Anything! Anything!" Andar gargled. "Anything!"

Those were the plaintive cries of a desperate man, one who would do anything, and say anything, to survive.

Andar would not help him. At best, he would leave Geon unmolested.

Still, Geon found himself removing the spear from Andar's throat. He knelt down and stretched out his hand.

White fire appeared over Geon's fingers. There was the sound of crunching, of clicking, as Andar's bones came back together and then sealed.

Andar breathed a sigh. His body became relaxed. The light returned to his eyes as he bathed in Geon's splendor.

And then he began to shout. "I will do it! I will do as you say! I promise.

"I am so sorry… I am so sorry, Geon. I don't know what came over me. I will not listen to Melara anymore."

His wife, Melara, had scolded him when he returned the

first time.

But Andar had proven himself weak.

As Andar ran back toward the city, shouting apologies, Geon knew he would never see him again. He knew Andar too well. He was feeble. He was an oaf. And he would not do what he said he would.

Why had Geon spared him? Only the gods knew.

HIGH CITY, THÉNAI

Khloë, for the first time in her life, stood before the magistrate, not as a supervisor, but as a criminal.

On the High City, amid the law courts, the magistrate sat upon a high bench, garbed in a chiton of scarlet cloth. Beside him were witnesses: Elena Kaiaphon, no longer with her false charm but with pursed lips and expressing all the callousness and coldness in her heart; and Taddaeos, the servant whom Khloë had struck.

In the pews, where some Thenoan citizens had gathered to watch, members of the governmental elite sat in judgment. Dioscouro, Phalco, everyone on the Council of War, all her old friends, had abandoned her. Now, she was a criminal, worthy only of scorn.

"Madness has gotten in to you!" Dioscouro had cried. "I want nothing to do with you! In all these years, you have only brought us trouble!"

In a sense, it was true, she thought, as she awaited the magistrate's judgment.

What good had her advice brought to the League's cause? They had never listened to her.

She had traveled all those miles, across the sea and deep into the interior. She had found Theron, sitting as king in a foreign land; and her old friend had refused to help her. That mission, as well, had been fruitless. Thénai had granted her citizenship; and what good had Khloë brought to her? Nothing, nothing at all.

"Khloë the Amazon, citizen of Thénai, daughter of Callorhoë," the magistrate said. "Explain yourself!"

When he spoke, she began to tremble. "I don't know… I can't explain." Tears formed in her eyes. "I am useless… worthless to the the League's cause."

"Why did you destroy Elena Kaiaphon's property?" the

magistrate said. "Why did you disturb the grave? Why did you strike her servant?"

"For Chillos," Khloë found herself muttering. "For Chillos' sake."

Elena's eyes grew wide.

But Khloë had become convinced that beyond her worthlessness, she was also mad. Everything she thought, everything she believed, was a lie. Surely, there was some explanation for Thestas' disappearance, and it had nothing to do with Elena Kaiaphon. Perhaps, Chillos was just a figment of her imagination. Perhaps, she had dreamed everything… made every bit of it up in her mind.

"You must pay, then, one-hundred *doukon* immediately," the magistrate said.

"I cannot pay," Khloë said. "I do not have the money." She had stowed away as much as twenty *doukon* from her salary on the Council of War. She had considered that a vast sum.

"Then you are sentenced to five years' hard labor," the magistrate said, "in the Mines of Sarxia."

Sarxia, far away, lay in the land of Khazidea. From there, the Thenoan League procured iron, gold and silver. A sentence in the mines was nothing less than a sentence to death. No one survived more than a year in such conditions. Whether by poisoning, or heat, or overwork, the Mines of Sarxia were not fit for human work. No mines were.

"Until the day you are shipped to your destination," the magistrate said, "I sentence you to house arrest. May Amara have mercy on you."

Elena was smiling, positively glowing. Taddaeos looked slightly less pleased.

To destroy a person's property earned you a light fine; but to destroy a rich woman's property—a Kaiaphon's property—why, that cost you your life.

~

For her holding cell, Khloë was led to a dark room in one of the House of the Archon's forgotten corners.

There was no plaster on the walls, allowing the bare brick face to be shown. She was given a gray, flea-bitten cot, and as soon as she entered, guards came to shut the door, and lock it.

She sat down on the cot; there were no chairs or furniture, no tables to speak of.

Then, inexplicably, she began to weep.

This was her reward, for trying to find Chillos. This was her reward for all the work on the Council of War, for attempting to guide the Thenoan League to victory.

Things would have turned out much better if life had not led her here. She was an amazon, and she did not belong. She thought of her mother, her father, her nine sisters and ten brothers. Her mother had encouraged her to seek her fortune in the human world; but her father had warned her against it.

"The human world is no place for one of us," old Laomer said.

Khloë listened more to her mother, considering her father a doddering fool. But it was he who had spoken wisdom; it was he who knew how things would turn out, how everything would slip from her grasp. It was he who sensed, all those years ago, that she would end up here: sentenced to death in the Mines of Sarxia, not a quick death but an agonizing and slow one. That was the price she had to pay for her piety, for her altruism… all because she cared so deeply for a poor boy whom no one else cared about.

Despite herself, amid her weeping, she began uttering something not unlike a prayer: "Let me go… let me go… free me…

let me run, and go back to Amazonia, where I belong…"

SPARE ROOM, HOUSE OF THE ARCHON, THÉNAI

Khloë awoke to the sound of creaking. Night had fallen, and the only light in her room was a lamp, burning brightly in the hands of Phalco.

"Khloë."

At the sound of his voice, she began to weep and shake, to bawl with a new force, until the sleeves of her dress were soaking wet.

She felt Phalco's hand on her shoulder. He had stooped down to comfort her.

"Khloë, Khloë… what have I done?" He sounded on the verge of tears himself. "If I hadn't told you…"

"It's no fault but my own," Khloë said. "I was trying… trying to find a boy. He'd been kidnapped." She broke down once more. "Ah… ah… I thought he was. I was probably crazy. I thought the Kaiaphons meant to sacrifice him. The Kaiaphons! Wealthy merchants! Citizens! It sounds so crazy when I say it aloud."

Phalco's touch became a light embrace. "It is not near as crazy as you imagine. In fact… I… I…" He began to weep as well.

"Do not worry for me," Khloë said. "I am an amazon. Amazons are strong. Humans perish in the Mines of Sarxia, but perhaps an amazon woman won't."

"Elena Kaiaphon," Phalco growled. "That she-wolf. She could have extended you mercy. She could have been gracious. But she wasn't. That she-wolf. That she-wolf!"

"What did you expect from an Old Believer?" Khloë said.

Perhaps, Phalco did not know that term. Perhaps, all he knew was what Elena Kaiaphon had demanded: that the statue remain in its place.

But at least it has been removed. At least it is gone… at least Amara's temple is no longer desecrated. What comfort was there in that? She would be a shade, floating along in gloom amid the River of Souls… or, if the philosophers were right, a worm-eaten carcass, a hunk of rotting flesh that would one day become dust. She wondered if the pain of work in the mines was too much to endure; if, at an opportune moment, she should rush off the High City and plunge to her death far below. Then she would avoid the back-breaking work that slowly destroyed her body, the poison air of the subterranean tunnels, the constant toil of pickaxe and hammer.

She wept with a new force, so strong she could no longer speak or think. The grief was filling her; death hovered above her like a baleful sword. She was a doomed woman, all because she strove to save a life, all because she tried so desperately hard to find Chillos.

No doubt, Chillos was already dead.

"I have the keys," Phalco said. "I can set you free."

"And then, they will know it was you," Khloë said. "And you'll be sent to the Mines of Sarxia, or worse."

What was worse than the Mines of Sarxia? What worse fate could there possibly be?

Phalco clutched her for a while. Eventually, he let go. He wiped the tears from his eyes. "Ah, Khloë… I am sorry… I am sorry…"

Phalco had told her about the Kaiaphons and their insistence of the statue's protection; but he bore no responsibility for Khloë's crime. Khloë had struck the Kaiaphons' servant. Khloë had ransacked the Kaiaphons' home. Khloë was ultimately responsible for it all.

"I heard…" Phalco mumbled under his breath. "I heard… the temple… drums…"

GREAT ARCTOS ROAD, OUTSIDE THE ISTEROI KINGDOM

When Axander and his army passed along the road, travelers unlucky enough to stand in their path fled in every direction.

At the head of so many hoplites and so much siege equipment, Axander was no doubt drawing the attention of the Thenoan League. But Taicho followed him; he had no choice. Bound in rope, he was marched along, with Pythio at his side. He was a captive, but he did not know why. His parents could not offer much; and if Axander demanded a ransom, would they ransom a cowardly son, one who had broken rank and fled in terror? No doubt, if word spread in Lornadion of Taicho's actions, his parents would become anathema to the town elders. Perhaps, they would be exiled themselves, for raising such a coward. He could imagine the Archon of Lornadion even now, scorning Taicho's father, blaming him.

A brownish river meandered through the valley, and on either side were fields of wheat, rows of beans and innumerable cattle pastures. At the river's shore were towns and villages, some walled and some unwalled. Here was the Isteroi Kingdom, and as Taicho marched, he heard the hoplites around him scoffing.

"Ah! Isteros!" they laughed. "We shall not expect too much strategy if they choose to fight!"

Others mocked the Isteroi for their red hair, their queer accents, and their overall ignorance. Taicho wondered if this reputation was well deserved; and he wondered what they thought of him and Pythio, both colonials from far across the sea.

Even the smallest village he saw in the Isteroi Kingdom had been larger than his home, Lornadion. What would these arrogant Kersicans say of Taicho and his family if they saw his small house and the olive grove he tended? Would they mock his mother, a woman of little learning, or his father, a man with only a glimmer of knowledge about agriculture?

Late in the afternoon, when the sun was setting and painting the land in red and gold, a trumpet sounded over the river valley, carrying through the hills, fields and forests.

Eventually, the thundering of hooves echoed, and a force of horsemen, hundreds strong, came riding toward them, south along the road.

The steeds they rode were mighty beasts, black and brown and white in color. Taicho had never seen horses so large. Their manes were flowing in the wind. Riding them were big brutes of men, dressed in leather jerkins and bronze helms. One rode with a flag in his hand—a red bear against a white field—and had no helmet to speak of. He was pallid and his red hair was tied in a ponytail. These were Isteroi, the barbarians whom Axander's men had so cruelly disparaged.

"Halt!" he shouted. "You travel through the land of the sovereign Isteroi! No men with swords and shields may pass through King Ydro's kingdom unannounced."

"Do not attempt to harm us!" Axander shouted. "A foe much stronger than you, the Free and Democratic Armies, tried and failed! They now float through the River of Souls; they are condemned to the underworld!"

The Isteroi flag-bearer did not seem intimidated. "Where do you seek to go? Wherever you go, you must have King Ydro's blessing! Else, you will face the sword."

Axander walked up to him, past the front lines of the Kersicans. The sun shone red on his headband.

He was left-handed; and even now, it was peculiar to see his sword in that hand, and the sling in his right.

"Is King Ydro a pious man?" Axander said. "Does he respect prophecy? Does he give credence to the Oracle and her decrees? To the Ruined Temple, now consecrated? Does he give respect to the holy gods and their mouthpiece?"

"King Ydro reveres the Oracle," the flag-bearer said. "It is not for you to question his piety."

"We seek to vanquish a monster who lives in defiance of the Oracle and her degrees!" Axander shouted. "A monstrous creature, a winged horror… he lurks outside your capital city, the very city of Arctos!

"If you are pious, you will let us through! We are none other than agents of the Oracle. We are her hands in the wider world. She dispatched us here, to destroy a monster that threatens Ydro's very kingdom."

The flag-bearer had begun to smile. "Ah!" he said. "Then you are welcome here! And know that you have more than the Oracle's favor as a reward.

"King Ydro offers fifty *doukon* if you will but kill the beast, clip his wings and bring them to him. He has been lurking outside the Royal City, preparing to strike; but even from afar, he has driven Arctos into turmoil and unrest.

"On behalf of His Royal Highness King Ydro, I grant you permission to pass along the road. Hasten to your destination. We will accompany you. Ydro will be glad to see you, Axander… you have the look of a hero about you, like Theron."

Axander grumbled something.

No hero liked to be compared to another. Taicho had heard of Theron. Even far away, in the colony of Lornadion, word of him had spread: a mighty man, with a club, in a lion's skin, had driven away the mighty southron empire. Songs were already sung of him, though he was far from dead.

The flag-bearer's smile had vanished. "I fear only a hero can defeat the monster… a hero greater than Theron… a hero like Phillipidēs."

What monster were they hunting? What kind of creature lay out there, beyond the farm fields, beyond the hills and the trees? Taicho shuddered at the thought.

A cold wind had begun to blow, and Pythio, standing beside Taicho, shivered in its embrace.

HIDDEN POND, OUTSIDE ARCTOS, ISTEROI KINGDOM

A spear of lightning lit up the sky, and thunder rolled, deafening in timbre. Rain was pouring, battering Geon, and the wind was like a spear of ice, piercing his tunic. Such a storm reminded him of the coming winter; sooner or later, the bitter cold would arrive, and Geon, without shelter, would take ill and perhaps die. The mission had taken on a new urgency. Sooner than Geon knew, it would become impossible to find Herodota, to draw her out of the warmth and safety of Arctos.

Geon rubbed his arms together, trying to keep warm, and took shelter underneath the boughs of a pine tree. Still, the rain continued, sometimes in showers and other times in a violent downpour. It seemed Father Winter intended to make his presence known. More storm clouds were rolling in, purple in color.

Back home, in his former state, Geon had looked forward to rain; the sound of it pattering on the rooftop had comforted him, sending him into a deep and comfortable sleep. Now, though a new power had filled him, he was completely exposed to the raw power of nature. The animals who normally greeted him at night had withdrawn to their dens and hiding places, fearing the thunder and lightning, the hail and the rain and the biting wind.

Geon was not invincible; a lightning strike or a falling tree, well placed, would kill him. Cowering under the tree, he despaired at the thought. If he could not complete his mission, if he could not lure Herodota and convince her to restore Amara's priesthood, the goddess and perhaps all the holy gods would be erased from memory. Thénai and its tributary towns would sink into darkness and ignorance; Amara would be forgotten. The desecration of the temple would remain; the stain of it would linger and never wash away. If Geon died, Amara's worship would be forgotten. If Geon died, Thénai would fall too. The fate of Eloesus, and perhaps the fate of the whole world, rested on Geon's shoulders. In his former life, he could never imagine such a burden. But the burden was his.

As the storm raged, he knelt in the moist ground. The pine needles, red and fallen from the boughs, formed a makeshift carpet. As the wind howled, he felt his wings stretch out behind him. In the night, his halo shone like a lantern. Though he was alone, and the animals had cowered in their burrows, he felt the presence of another. He stood up and wandered out of the trees' protection. At the rocky shore of the pond, he began to peer into the water. The wind was forming ripples, but against the blackness he saw a light forming, a light that was not his own: a light, pale blue in color, that was growing in size.

The light became an image, like a window. There in the pond, Geon saw a woman tossing and turning in her bed. She had a shaved head and her black wig had been cast aside; it lay on the floor beside her. This was Herodota he was seeing, in the midst of a troubled sleep.

Geon shut his eyes; he willed himself to enter her dream.

~

When Geon met her, she was naked, holding a cloth to cover her breasts and groin. Fire surrounded her, and the air was thick with the scent of smoke and burning flesh.

He recognized this place instantly; this was the field outside Thénai of many months ago. This was Thénai's countryside just after the Kersicans had put the city to the sword; they had turned the grassland and pastures into a waking hell.

This was Thénai as Herodota imagined it still was. This was the Thénai Herodota had fled, in the middle of the night, when her sister priestesses had fallen to the sword. This was the Thénai Herodota had wept for, the one she still prayed and supplicated for. This was her old home.

"Herodota!" Geon shouted, and his voice was like the voice of a god, carrying above the roar of the flames, filling not just the ear but the mind as well, reverberating through the soul and psyche.

Herodota staggered backward. There were tears in her eyes, tears of anger. "Who are you?" she shouted. "*What* are you?"

Geon sensed her heart; she was full of wrath at Amara and at the holy gods, at what they had allowed to happen. There was no doubt in her but only anger, anger at Amara's cruelty, anger at the gods' capriciousness. "Herodota. You must come to Hidden Pond!" Geon shouted, but his voice had returned to normal and would not carry above the raging inferno.

Herodota turned away from him. She crossed her arms. Her hands were shaking. "What have you done, O gods? What have you allowed to happen? My sisters… they are dead! How devout were they, how attendant to the rituals and the ceremonies? And yet, you allowed the barbarians to cut them down! You betrayed your worshipers. You betrayed the city you claimed to love. You betrayed the pious!"

"Herodota!" Geon shouted, but his voice had been reduced to a whisper; no matter how much he tried to shout, what came out was soft and inaudible. "Herodota! Herodota!" It was no use; this would fail as well. Herodota would never come. He would never see her. He would never convince her to return to Thénai. The rituals and mysteries of Amara would be forgotten. In time, they would perish from memory; and the temple on the High City would become a haunt of wild animals, a place of desecration and desolation.

"Herodota!" Geon shouted. "*Herodota!*" At last his voice carried, deafening, thundering, reverberating, a message of the gods. "Come to me. Come to Hidden Pond. And I will tell you everything... why the gods allowed your friends to die... why the gods allowed your city to fall."

Herodota snapped back towards her, tears in her eyes, the red of the fire reflecting in her gaze. "No... No... I will not go anywhere... this is, after all, just a dream..."

The air and the flame began to waver, like the canvas of a painting. The dream was fading.

"No! Come to Hidden Pond!" Geon shouted. "This is more than a dream!"

~

When Geon came to his senses once more, the rain had faded to a drizzle. Some of the clouds had dispersed; the air was cool, and the rosy light of dawn illumined Hidden Pond. Herodota was nowhere to be seen; she could not be lured, she could not be convinced. She would not come. The memory of Amara and all the holy gods would perish from the earth; and darkness and ignorance would fall over the whole world.

GREAT ARCTOS ROAD, ISTEROI KINGDOM

Axander was a tough marcher.

Taicho was woken up before dawn, given a small ration of waybread and a bit of water. Then they marched for hours, taking only a brief break, and ceasing their labor at dusk.

The Isteroi Kingdom was grander than anything back home, far to the west in the land of Dys. To great cities such as Thénai and Kersepoli, the Isteroi Kingdom was a backwater, a land of freckled, redheaded barbarians with only a tenuous claim to Eloesian ethnicity. But the villages were grander than Lornadion, and connecting them all were vast roads paved white, dotted with statues and monuments of white marble. Compared to Dys, it was land of marvel and splendor.

Late in the day, Axander and his men crossed a high hill. Below them, at the shore of the river, was a vast city surrounded by mighty walls. The smoke of habitation rose up above it.

"Here!" the Isteroi guide shouted. "Welcome to the Royal City. But ye may not enter until you clip the wings of the monster. Then Axander may bring them to King Ydro and collect his reward."

Taicho had been led all this way; as a captive, for what purpose, he did not know. But he would fall or he would triumph with Axander's army. He had no choice.

"Where was he last seen?" Axander said.

"Why," the guide said, "in a sacred pond. It was left untouched by the priests; it is favored of Seladora, mother of nymphs. And the monster desecrated it with its presence. Even swam within its waters—an offense against god and man. Come. I will show you the way. Perhaps, I will fight alongside you."

HIDDEN POND, OUTSIDE ARCTOS, ISTEROI KINGDOM

A small cluster of trees surrounded the pond, but the pond was empty; there was no sign of the monster anywhere. But a cluster of pine boughs formed a makeshift hut near the shore of the pond, and amid the dirt and stones, Taicho noted small crumbs, bits of discarded waybread that the birds—perhaps out of fear—had not touched.

This "monster" did not live in a cave, but in a house of his own making, like a human. The "monster" did not feed on the flesh of men or animals, but on waybread. What kind of monster was this? Perhaps, it was a monster very much like Taicho, or Pythio, or Axander. Perhaps, it was a man of great power—a hero, forsaken and misunderstood. Perhaps, he was not so different from Axander, only in intent.

Axander was mumbling curses under his breath. "He fled! He fled!" He ground the dirt underneath his sandal and flexed his grip around his shortsword.

"My lord! My lord!" one of the hoplites.

Hoplites calling their leader "lord" was hard for Taicho to get used to.

"Come with me!" the hoplite continued. "Over here!"

They fled through the woods.

Down a hill, amid the farm fields, at the shore of the river's brown waters, a figure of light, wreathed in splendor, dallied near the shore. From such a distance, Taicho could not distinguish his features or see his face. But the sight of him filled his heart with warmth and peace. For once, he no longer worried about what

Mother and Father and the Council of Elders back in Lornadion would think. For once, he no longer felt the shame of cowardice, and the burden of guilt. For once, all his problems seemed petty. All that mattered was the splendid light, and the warmth working its way through Taicho's heart.

RIVER ISTER, OUTSIDE ARCTOS

If Geon swam through the river, he could make it to Arctos' port. There, in the port, was a house with lattice windows; and behind those lattice windows was the one he sought, the one who was slipping away from him: Herodota. It was clear winter was coming. Time was slipping away from him. No one would help him. If he had to risk death, if he had to storm into the city and snatch Herodota away then, why, that was exactly what he would do.

He turned, and the wind caught in his wings, blowing him a short distance forward.

High above him on a hill, a number of hoplites were approaching, as many as a thousand, and several hundred Isteroi cavalry. Beside them, on great wheels, were catapults bearing stones and ballistae loaded with javelins. At the fore of them was a man with his brown hair held up in a headband. He was dressed lightly, and wore no helm or breastplate. In his left hand he held a sword; in his right a sling.

Geon sensed instantly his purpose; that he had been sent from the Oracle, all for the purpose of killing Geon and bringing back his head. This man was her agent; he was her hand in the world of mortals.

The Oracle had lost control of Theron; but this man, bearing the sword in his left hand and the sling in his right, he was her slave… he was firmly under her thumb.

All this was happening because Geon refused to bend her knee and do her bidding. He was at risk of death because he saw the Oracle for who she was: a dark-hearted murderess, cold-hearted, cold-blooded, calculating, thinking of nothing except her own power.

Geon held up the Spear of Pegara, and bore her shield to his breast. He would stand his ground; he would not relent. If he perished here, by the shore of the River Ister, he would perish fighting, having given all to his quest. Perhaps, Herodota would hear of his bravery, and reconsider bitterness; perhaps, she would return to Amara's service with a vengeance, and her old zeal would be restored.

RIVER ISTER, OUTSIDE ARCTOS

Here he was: Axander's prey.

Axander took stock of him as he descended the hill.

He was not as the Oracle had described him, or as Axander had imagined.

A halo of frosty blue light crowned his head. His body, in the dim dusk, seemed wreathed in light, so that he gave off a glow. His spear and shield shimmered. His eyes were bright blue, the color of his halo; and from him warmth and peace seemed to radiate, a feeling that did not calm Axander but angered him.

My mission is just, Axander swore. *Any hero would do the same.*

Here, in the hills outside Arctos, in the barbaric Isteroi Kingdom, this heavenly creature would perish. Axander would cast him down from his lofty heights; he would bring him back down to earth.

Geon, the Monster of Isteros, would soon meet his fate.

RIVER ISTER, OUTSIDE ARCTOS

Would they really harm him, Taicho wondered.

Taicho had never seen a creature of such beauty and brilliance, such celestial glory. This creature did not belong on the earth; he belonged in the clouds with the birds and the cupids. Taicho would not harm him, no matter how much Axander poked and prodded. He would rather die than harm this Geon. He stood there and let the glory wash over him, banishing the darkness and bitterness from his heart.

RIVER ISTER, ARCTOS

Pythio did not know what to think of Geon; he had never seen such a creature, not even in paintings or mosaics. He had never heard of such a creature in stories or in songs. But here he was, sporting bright swan-like wings, radiating light and glory.

He began to wonder... should he tell Axander his secret? Should he speak to Taicho, the barbarian he had deigned to ignore?

RIVER ISTER, OUTSIDE ARCTOS

The battle came like a flood, rushing, overpowering, unrelenting.

The ballistae were let loose; javelins came hurtling toward Geon, grazing his wings, but he dodged each one. Catapults rained stones like thunderbolts, but they were clumsy and missed each time.

A sick expression was on Axander's face, hungry, greedy, desperate for silver and gold, desperate for the Oracle's approval, desperate for blood.

Axander hurled a stone with a sling, and for once, Geon was hit; the stone crushed his jaw and sent a tooth flying.

Geon could no longer merely defend himself; he had to attack. He did not delight in spilling blood, but he would not offer himself as a sacrifice. He would fight back.

Axander hurled another stone, and it struck home, crushing a rib.

Geon charged, pitching back his spear, and swept it towards Axander, but Axander nimbly dodged and fell backward. Geon slammed the Shield of Pegara into Axander's face and he went flying.

One by one Geon fell upon the hoplites, plunging his spear into their hearts, one, two, three, four, five.

Some began to creep backward; one hoplite dropped his shield and fled.

Geon turned his wrath upon the ballistae and catapults.

He struck a ballista with the Shield of Pegara, and it collapsed into a pile of wood timbers. He struck a catapult to his left and it fell to pieces and rubble.

The greed and hunger in Axander's eyes had faded, giving way to panic, to fear.

The white light of Geon's splendor was in Axander's eyes. He had become an avenger and not a healer, a clenched fist and not an open hand.

The hoplites who survived broke rank and fled in every direction.

Axander stumbled backward a moment, eyes wide, full of fear, full of terror. At last he, as well, fled from Geon's presence.

Geon did not pursue him. He had learned his lesson. He had learned not to interfere in the gods' work. He had learned that even heroes were mortal, that the Oracles' power was limited; that she had made a mistake when she had raised him. No hero would halt Geon's advance. No hero would foil Geon's plans.

He would find Herodota, one way or another. He would restore the priesthood, and no power on earth, or in the heavens or in the underworld, could stop him.

HIDDEN POND, ISTEROI KINGDOM

Geon returned to his old haunt that night. His jaw was broken and bleeding, and he could scarcely walk, only stagger, with the pain in his ribs.

It was a painful reminder that he was mortal. If Axander had not fled in terror, perhaps he would have accomplished his mission; he would have brought the Oracle's enemy low.

But he *had* fled in terror, and Geon was safe, for now, but demoralized.

He could not swim in this state; he could not enter the city. Winter would fall, and Herodota would remain in utter despair.

Against the sound of the night birds and the chirp of the crickets, shouting arose, and Geon recognized the voice instantly.

It was Andar.

Geon grabbed the Sword and Shield of Pegara where they lay. He winced in pain as he held them up. In such a weakened state, perhaps Andar would be able to overcome him.

Andar emerged through the thicket of pines and cypress trees. But he was not alone.

A woman was there, dressed in blue, with a wig of black hair on her head.

"I did as I promised," Andar was saying, with tears in his eyes. "I did as I promised! Here she is. Herodota… Herodota, the priest."

SPARE ROOM, HOUSE OF THE ARCHON, THÉNAI

Khloë woke with a start. Outside, the night was thick and heavy, but the silence was not complete.

She heard a pounding, so faint she thought it might be in her imagination. It was rhythmic, steady… like drums.

That was what had woken her. What could it be?

Here, in her makeshift prison, she had spent countless nights weeping. She had imagined things before. She had, after all, imagined that Phalco could be trusted, that he was truly a friend. She had imagined Dioscouro had good intentions and a good heart. She had imagined that she was a valuable member of the Council of War, that her advice and her words were respected and honored. She had imagined many things over these days, and months, and weeks, and years.

She held her breath and shut her eyes, trying to block out her thoughts, her preconceived notions, everything but the silence around her.

And the drums persisted, so faint they were barely audible, a rhythmic pounding no louder than a rock falling to the floor.

She stood up and leapt up to the window, grabbing the iron bars in her hand.

The night was dark, but there were lights in the windows of Amara's temple, the temple that—according to Dioscouro—was without a priesthood and without use.

Someone was inside the supposedly empty temple, and the sound of drums were coming from within.

"Damn it all," Khloë breathed. She dropped back down.

Why was the temple open? Why were lamps burning inside? Why was the sound of music emanating from it, music that was not Amara's?

She did not care if they put her to death. "I will find out." She made a vow to herself, right then. She promised to Amara and the holy gods that she would avenge them, no matter what occurred. She would break free from this prison, even if it cost her her life.

Starting from one end of the room, she charged to the other, ending into a violent kick to the door. The hinges buckled, and the wood around them splintered.

She kicked again, and the door lurched forward, unusable.

"What are you doing?" The shout of Phalco echoed, but she gave his voice and command no heed.

She kicked again and the door came crashing off its hinges. It fell with a thunderous clap onto the hallway outside.

Phalco came rushing toward her. She kicked him and sent him to the floor.

She hobbled, still in her binds over to him.

She clawed his dagger out of its sheath. With her teeth, she slowly began to cut away at her binds. At last they burst apart, and with her hands untied, freed her legs as well.

"Thank you." She spat at Phalco and rushed down the hall.

~

After recovering her sabers, she charged out of the House of the Archon, heedless of her fate. Guards chased her but she did not care, she fled, out of the prison wing, out of the corridor, and out the front door.

She stopped a moment before the temple's open doors. The sound of drums was louder than ever, clearly not in her head.

The High City was empty and open, silent save for the drums.

She turned to the guards pursuing her.

"Stop!" she shouted. "Halt! Or will you partake in the sacrilege? Will you allow the holy temple to be desecrated?"

She ran toward the temple's open doors, and the guards did not chase after her.

~

She entered the sanctuary; the abominable statue was gone, as Dioscouro had promised. It had been crudely cut from its pedestal, and only chipped traces of bronze feet remained.

The drums were coming from around the corner, from the inmost part of the temple, the Inner Shrine where the holy rituals of Amara had once been performed.

A cold feeling settled over Khloë as she ran through the dimly lit corridors and rooms.

All the temple's treasures had been pilfered: the chambers and cupboards were bare, and all the gold and silver was gone. The statues and reliquaries had been stolen, no doubt melted into their component parts of precious metals and gems. Such a sacrilege had never taken place before, in all Eloesian history, but here it was, and here Khloë was, in the center of it.

The door to the Inner Shrine was shut, but she could hear chants and singing beyond it, and the sound of a pounding drum.

She kicked it open and a scream rang out.

In the Inner Shrine, torches were burning, torches and lamps and lanterns, some held, some propped up, some fixed to the walls.

~

Dozens of men and women stood there, dressed in black

hoods. They continued their chanting; none had heard Khloë over the sound of the music and the ecstasy of the ritual.

The statue had not been moved away; it had been hidden from sight.

It stood there, in the midst of the Inner Shrine, an abomination, a terror. Its three heads were locked in a silent scream. Its scorpion-like body had lifelike detail. Six pairs of bat wings stretched to the top of the Inner Shrine's ceiling. Khloë wondered how they had hauled it inside.

Before the monstrous statue was an altar, and to the altar a boy had been tied. It had to be Chillos.

Khloë let out a wail.

Standing before Chillos, with a ritual knife, was Elena Kaiaphon. Her black hood was lowered, baring her identity for all to see.

The altar was already stained with blood.

An eviscerated Thestas lay to its side, his chest carved open and hollow.

"Ya Kronos! Ya Kronos!" Elena Kaiaphon sang.

"Ya Kronos! Ya Kronos!" the crowd chanted back, and the drum pounded once more.

The drummer wore a mask of scales, giving him a reptilian appearance. A hammer was in his hand; he struck the drum and its timbre filled the Inner Shrine once more.

"Ya Kronos! Ya Kronos!" Elena Kaiaphon sang.

"Ya Kronos! Ya Kronos!" the crowd chanted again.

"O blessed Kronos, Lord of the World, suffering in chains, may you be freed from your prison!" Elena Kaiaphon sang.

"Ya Kronos! Ya Kronos!" the crowd sang.

"Thestas' life is yours; but it is this Chillos who is most precious in your sight!" Elena continued.

"Ya Kronos! Ya Kronos!"

"May this offering grant us your favor!" Elena said. "Bless the Thenoan League! Destroy its enemies! Banish the Kersican League from existence, and bring it to rubble!"

"Ya Kronos! Ya Kronos!"

"Send your favor upon the Free and Democratic Armies!" Elena shouted. "Let the plans of the Kersican League fail. Curse them and vanquish them! Burn them! Crush them! Turn them to dust in your hand!"

Horror filled Khloë, horror she could not express, horror no one could understand. For a while she stood there, too stunned and disgusted to act. All these men and women, hiding themselves behind hoods, had walked in Thénai without their neighbors knowing. Behind a facade of normality, they hid their monstrous hearts.

Kronos, the ancient enemy of Eloesus, would not stoop to help anyone except himself. They were as foolish as they were cruel; and as Khloë beheld Chillos' helpless body, she drew her sabers and let out a shout: "Avast! For Amara!"

At last, Elena took notice of her. Her eyes bulged and her mouth lay agape for a moment. Wrath, wrath like Khloë had never seen before, filled Elena's eyes. "Amazon! Amazon! You are bound for Sarxia. You do not belong here! Not in Eloesus! Not even in the human world."

For once, an Old Believer had spoken truth.

Khloë charged, and the Old Believers panicked, turning back and running in every direction. Only Elena stood there, firm and unyielding, the sacrificial dagger still in her hands.

"Amazon!" Elena said. "My brother perished. And now you will kill me as well… a fellow traveler… a fellow patriot."

"You are no patriot," Khloë said.

She rushed Elena, and Elena broke off, dashing out of the room. Khloë did not pursue her.

Chillos was crying; he had survived his ordeal, but Thestas the insurrectionist lay dead beside him in a pool of blood, his chest carved up, his innards removed. The Old God had sated a little of its hunger, but what it desired most had escaped from it.

With her saber, Khloë slashed Chillos' binds. She would return him to his parents this very night.

~

Dozens of hoplites awaited her when she exited the temple. She had Chillos in hand, dressed in nothing but his underclothes. Out of the crowd of soldiers, dressed in helmets, breastplates and capes, she made out a man in a white chiton and a blue sash. This was the demiarch Teucer, Speaker of the Assembly.

"Lay down your arms, criminal!" Teucer said.

Khloë dropped the saber in her right hand and let go of Chillos.

The little boy went running toward the crowd, crying and screaming.

"Who is this boy?" Teucer growled.

"Why don't you ask Elena Kaiaphon?" Khloë answered.

HELĒMON AND KORË
A FABLE

A poor girl named Korë came to the Temple of Alabastros, begging for rescue. She was starving and suffering from disease; death stalked her, a black sword hovering above her and ready to strike. She asked the gods that the great hero Helēmon would come to rescue her.

That night Helēmon returned to the city from a far country, and the girl Korë threw herself upon him, begging him to rescue her from her poverty and her illness.

"I am sorry," Helēmon told her. "I cannot help you. The gods have laid this poverty and illness on you, and none can stand against their decrees."

Korë wept bitterly as he walked away, for she knew the truth of his words: what the gods determine, none can thwart.

—Amalchio

HIDDEN POND, OUTSIDE ARCTOS, ISTEROI KINGDOM

Herodota stood there in the light of Geon's wings, in the radiance of his splendor. There were tears in her eyes, and Andar stood there, a little way off, saying nothing.

"What are you?" Herodota asked. "Are you from above?"

Her eyes inclined to the night sky.

But Geon shook his head. "I am just a man," he said, "a man from Thénai. I am a Thenoan like you."

"No, no," Herodota said, "you are not like me. And you are not from this world. If you cannot see it, you are blind."

Andar began to walk away, toward the lights of the city. His quest was complete.

"Andar," Geon said, and his voice carried. "Where are you going?"

Andar turned to face him, and Geon's light illuminated his bright red hair, his brilliant blue eyes. "I have done as you wished," he said. "Now, I must go home."

"You will not aid the mission?" Geon said. "You will not help restore Amara's priesthood?"

Andar shook his head. The light illuminated tears forming in his eyes. "I have a wife... children..."

But Geon sensed his future; he could see it as if it were written in a parchment scroll. His wife and his children would leave him soon. Dark days awaited Andar, but he did not know, though he had begun to suspect. "Farewell," Geon said. "It is your choice, Andar."

Soon, his shadowy form had disappeared into the night,

leaving Herodota and Geon alone.

~

A cold wind was blowing, rustling the leaves of the trees and forming ripples in the waters of the pond.

Herodota had taken a seat by the shore. She had removed her wig of black hair and set it by her side, baring her bald head for all to see.

Of all the customs of the priesthood of Amara, the shaving of the head had always struck Geon as oddest. Instead of their own hair, they wore black-dyed wigs, tied in curls and tresses. Each priestess had the same blue gown, the same hair, so that they looked identical from a distance.

Geon thought of all the sisters Herodota had lost, all the women whom she had served alongside, who now were dead. They had fallen to the treacherous southrons' scimitars and swords. They had fallen at the hands of foreigners, having dedicated their lives to a goddess who in their minds had been powerless to save them.

Here Herodota was, the only survivor, the only one of her sisters who had endured to the end, who had escaped the ravages of the war. She was the last of Amara's servants in the mortal world, the last who knew the rituals, the last who knew how to restore the temple and return the memory of the goddess to the human realm. The customs were not written down; they were remembered by heart.

~

"Why," Herodota was murmuring amid the silence of the night. "Why, why why… Eudora… Kirillia.. Ainopë… Calliopë… they are dead. They are dead! My sisters, murdered in the cruelest of ways…"

"Why?" Geon repeated. "I do not know why. I do not know. They are dead, Herodota, but you were spared. You have a task ahead of you. Thénai has been liberated. It lies in safety. And it is up to you to sanctify the temple… to restore the priesthood. You are the only one who can."

Herodota wiped the tears from her eyes. "I will not. I cannot. I cannot do anything for Amara or the holy gods. They betrayed my sisters. They allowed Thénai to fall. They allowed the city to be butchered. They are uncaring, or they are powerless.

"I will not do it! I swear, on my life, I will not do it."

But her tone did not seem certain. When Geon peered into the woman's eyes, he saw a broken woman, one who was devastated by what she had seen, whose faith had been shaken, whose life had been uprooted and destroyed. She had faced scorn and ill favor in Arctos, in part for being a refugee, in part for being a priestess of Amara in a city that revered Tyros lord of war.

Yet she had not lost all her devotion, and despite the blackness that filled her, the darkness and gloom that consumed her, there was a little spark of hope left, one that Geon intended to kindle.

LAW COURTS, HIGH CITY, THÉNAI

Khloë knelt before the magistrate and crossed her arms over her chest. "Mercy," she said.

She had presented all the evidence she could.

The magistrate was perched above her, sitting on his pedestal, wearing a red chiton over his chest. His hair was gray, reflecting in the brightness of the morning sun.

"Khloë the Amazon, citizen of Thénai, daughter of Callorhoë," the magistrate said, "I have determined a great injustice has been wrought upon you. You are to be commended for attempting to save the lost child. I remove the sentence of guilt, and its accordant punishment! Khloë, I free you. The Mines of Sarxia are no place for you. Go in liberty, and in peace."

Khloë breathed a sigh of relief, and with that exhale all the worry and torment of prior days and weeks seemed to leave with it. She could finally relax again; she could finally regain her bearings, and think with clarity on her next move. Did she belong in Thénai? She had begun to doubt.

Far below, in the city, bells began to ring, bells she recognized, bells that indicated the House of Assembly was in session.

As a free woman, now, and still a member of the government, it was her duty to attend, though there was nothing less she wanted to do. She had seen Thénai's governing elite for what they were; she had watched them betray her. But for the time being, for today, and the next few days, she would do her civic duty.

~

When Khloë entered the main hall of the House of Assembly, a floor of marble made to look like a laurel wreath, demiarchs were irate and shouting.

Dioscouro stood there, his hands bound in rope, flanked by two hoplites who were not his guards.

Dioscouro was ashen faced, and his lips were trembling. Khloë had never seen him afraid before.

The hundreds of demiarchs, and hundreds of delegates from the tributary cities, were raising their fists, some red-faced with anger.

At last, Teucer, Speaker of the Assembly, strode forward. "Silence!" he shouted. Dioscouro refused to look at him. "Shouted words will help nothing! Shouted words will not bring justice! Only our actions will!"

The House of Assembly grew hushed.

Teucer raised his hand. "Dioscouro, son of Thelemos, you are a Thenoan citizen but you shall face a fair trial!

"You lied to the House of Assembly! You claimed the abominable statue had been removed, but instead it was transported to the Inner Shrine and left alone!"

Dioscouro was turned to face him, but he said nothing. His hands and arms were shaking; he looked pitiful now, a poor shadow of what he once had been. No longer was he the bold, brash archon, but a criminal receiving his due.

"You are not above the law, Dioscouro!" Oinos continued. "I make a motion to those assembled here, to strip Dioscouro, son of Thelemos, of his title, to purge his name from the city's memory, to hold new elections and declare a new archon! Moreover, the abominable statue must be removed at once!"

Khloë watched from the shadows as the vote was taken: in the end, every demiarch and delegate present voted aye; and Dioscouro was half-dragged, half-carried away, weeping and shrieking. His tenure had brought Thénai back from the brink, but it had ended in ignominy and disgrace.

When Khloë left the House of Assembly, it was almost dusk. Just outside, a vast crowd was gathering, and growing in number each moment. Thousands of men and women had assembled. Some were growling among themselves; others shouting. Khloë could sense the tension even where she stood.

Something baleful was about to occur; something dreadful that would rock the city to its core.

OUTSIDE ARCTOS, ISTEROI KINGDOM

Taicho had fled only a little while before Axander had caught up to him.

He and a dozen hoplites had regathered after fleeing from the heavenly creature.

Later in the day, they found Pythio wandering in the fields.

Axander seemed crestfallen; the wind seemed to have been taken out from under him. He had failed. He had never experienced failure before, but here it was; and it tasted as bitter as he feared.

Taicho, on the other hand, knew failure all too well. He had followed Pythio, his shield-mate, in a cowardly retreat. He did not know if death awaited him in Lornadion, but he surely deserved it.

Axander and the hoplites re-bound Pythio's hands, tying them so tight his flesh bulged.

"Ah!" Pythio said. "My lords! Please! I won't run. *Ah!*"

"Tell me, Taicho." Axander had turned to face him. "Why shouldn't I end you right now?"

He was taking out his failure on his captives. So be it.

"Ehrm," Taicho began, "I… I am a great warrior."

Axander laughed so hard, tears began to form in his eyes. He wiped the moisture with his sleeve, but soon his cheerful demeanor had vanished. "I will put you to death at sundown. You will slow us down."

But where was Axander going? Did he intend to fight the creature again? Why would he, after he had faltered with hundreds of hoplites backing him up, and catapults and ballistae whose projectiles had proven useless? No, he was going somewhere else, and Taicho did not know where.

"You," Axander pointed.

"Pythio," he said. Apparently, Axander had already forgotten the young man's name.

"Why shouldn't I execute you alongside this useless oaf?" Axander said.

"You would do well not to kill either of us," Pythio said. "You will be a rich man if you do not... a dead man if you do."

Taicho had never heard Pythio speak so much before. His accent became evident, yapping, southron in character.

Axander smiled; he appeared amused, despite the graveness of the situation. Who knew where the so-called "monster" lurked and how wrathful the Oracle would be?

"You speak boldly, captive," Axander said. "Tell me why you are a threat to me."

"My father is none other than the King of Khazidea," Pythio said, "and I can prove it."

What a great liar, Taicho thought. He had spoken those words as if he truly believed them, as if they were true.

Axander laughed aloud.

"My father is a king," Pythio insisted, "with a host of soldiers fighting in his name. He is fabulously wealthy... wealthier than all of Thénai. To him, this land is a nest of barbarians... but I heard of the Thenoan League's struggle for liberty... for democracy... and I decided to fight. I decided to enlist. And I told no one who I was.

"This young man here, who calls himself Taicho... he is none other than my father's cupbearer. If you harm a hair on his head, you will hear from my father, and it won't end well for you."

The mood changed.

Pythio sounded convincing. Taicho almost believed. Pythio lied about Taicho; but did he speak the truth about all else?

Axander was no longer laughing.

"Do you wish ten talents in gold and silver for our ransom,"

Pythio said, "or do you want the knife of one of my father's Anakhil in your throat?"

"You are boastful," Axander said, "and you are delusional, too, if you think a Khazidean barbarian can overcome a hero."

"The hero Theron came to my father's land," Pythio said, "and he defeated the Carceran Lion; but he did not escape without scars. Heroes are mortal. Heroes can die."

At the words, Pythio tore the top of his tunic away, revealing his bare chest. There, a diamond necklace twinkled in the sunlight, a necklace no peasant or common soldier could possibly afford. The gold was formed in the shape of an egret, with two diamonds forming its eyes.

On Pythio's dark chest, Khazidean writing was tattooed in black ink—pictograms resembling various animals and manmade objects. If this did not convince Axander nothing would; but now Taicho truly believed.

Over all these days and weeks, he had been marching alongside a prince, the son of a rich and powerful king. No wonder he had kept to himself. No wonder he had not deigned to speak to Taicho, or befriend him. He considered himself far above them all.

For a while, Axander said nothing; the truth was dawning on him, faster and more furiously than he could have imagined. "Ah," he said at last, "Pythio. We have a problem. There is no way to get you home."

FIELDS, BORDER OF THENOA AND THE ISTEROI KINGDOM

In the night, Axander led Pythio and Taicho away.

Axander had changed. Now, it seemed to him, imperative that he return Pythio for a ransom. In the end, it seemed even heroes could be swayed by gold.

"We must send a message to your father," Axander began to murmur. "But how? I shall take you back to Kersepoli!"

"No," Pythio said. "No, no… that will not work at all. If you are to be believed, a trusted servant must send the letter.

"My guardian Udu is waiting behind in Thénai. If you send a mere letter, you will not be believed."

Axander stared at Pythio a while, gritting his teeth together. Perhaps, he realized the truth of his words. Why would the King of Thénai believe a letter sent by a stranger?

"You are wily," Axander said, "and you wish to escape. We go to Kersepoli."

He laid hold of the necklace around Pythio's chest, then removed it.

He smiled. "To Kersepoli we go. We send your father the proof he needs. And if he does not listen, then, why, he will lose a son, and he will lose a cupbearer."

Axander turned and walked south, toward the road. They would head to the heart of enemy territory, to the place Taicho dreaded above all.

He recalled the lessons he'd been taught in Lornadion's town square, of how Kersepoli would enslave free Eloesians and turn them into the subhuman "Elehoi." Kersepoli, the capital and namesake of the Kersican League, was no place for a Free and Democratic soldier. But he had no choice but to go there.

CITY SQUARE, THÉNAI

The crowd, gathering in City Square, had grown so numerous that it spilled out into the network of streets. They had begun to shout words that turned into slogans: "Long live Dioscouro! Long live Dioscouro!"

Khloë, hiding away in the shadows, unable to return home, could sense the tension, threatening to spill over.

When the demiarchs voted to remove the archon, they had not quite clearly thought it all out.

Even Khloë, seeing Dioscouro for the slimy serpent he was, had forgotten his widespread popularity with the people, both poor and rich.

The City of Thénai had not demanded another election; but an election they would get, and Dioscouro would not be one of their choices.

As the angry shouts grew in volume, and became more unified, Khloë began to push her way roughly through the crowd, hauling the members of the mob away, but she could not act quickly enough.

"There is that amazon!" she heard someone snap. A hand grabbed at her, and she pushed faster and more furiously, knocking men and women aside.

She reached the ramp to the High City just before the violence erupted.

From a great height, she watched as the crowd began to surround the House of Assembly.

Hoplites were posted outside its doors, but Khloë knew from experience that many demiarchs remained inside, together with politarchs and servants that never left.

Khloë could hear the crowd, carrying throughout the city, angry shouts that—together—formed a deafening cacophony.

The crowds tried to swarm the House of Assembly, and the hoplites responded.

From the high perch, Khloë watched as a spear pierced one of the protesters' chests.

The crowd converged with a new fierceness.

Hoplites were approaching from the barracks on the west side of the city.

A veritable battle was starting. Bloodshed would consume the city. And, for now, the abominable statue which started it all would remain, defiling the holy Inner Sanctuary.

Perhaps, Khloë told herself, *I will remove it myself. I will pull it from its place and cast it off the High City myself.*

As blood was shed far below, and the government—for the first time in a long time—used deadly force against citizens, Khloë ran up the ramp of the High City toward her old quarters, the only place that was safe.

~

Before she reached the House of the Archon, Phalco stopped her.

He was dressed fully in the breastplate and the horsehair-crested helm of a hoplite.

"Khloë!" he said through his visor. "Run! The other way!"

Only then, did she realize the House of the Archon was in flames, a raging inferno that was consuming its roof and walls.

Khloë stood there a moment, taken aback, horrified at the sight of it.

"I— I— what happened?" Khloë said. "What happened?"

Through the haze and smoke, a number of dark shapes became visible, dressed in black robes.

Elena Kaiaphon was not among them; she had been sent

to City Prison.

Where could she escape the Old Believers? Where could she escape their abominable statue? What was left for her? How could she find refuge?

She followed Phalco at a sprint, but soon even he stopped. "What is happening?" he said.

"The people!" Khloë said. "The people have risen up! Dioscouro has been removed from his office…

"The people love him, despite it all. They love him!"

Thénai was at war; it had powerful enemies, acting in concert against it. Without unity, without strength, without cohesion, it would fall. But now Khloë saw Thénai's gravest enemy was not the Kersican League or the southrons; it was herself.

She cursed the work she had done. She cursed all she had done to save the Thenoan League. She cursed herself for ever hopping on that ship, for ever trying to seek her fortunes in the realm of humanity.

Trapped between the overrun High City on one hand and the bloody battle in the streets below, Khloë stood shoulder to shoulder with Phalco, unable to move, unable to act.

HILL COUNTRY, THENOA

The night was dark, and clouds veiled the moon.

Axander was marching, with Pythio and Taicho ahead of him.

A cold wind was blowing when earth began to shake beneath their feet.

Pythio fell first, hitting his bottom and losing a sandal in the process.

Taicho fell flat-faced to the ground. Only Axander remained firm.

The earth was ripped open before them; a crack opened up in the soil, and then another. A patchwork spiderweb of fissures burst into existence, and the hills themselves were shaken.

Taicho was no priest. He did not know the mysteries or rites, but he knew such an earthquake was a bad omen, the symbol of something dreadful entering the world.

"Gods help us!" Taicho breathed, but Axander was shouting.

"Forward! Forward!" he cried. "Kersepoli awaits."

HIDDEN POND, OUTSIDE ARCTOS, ISTEROI KINGDOM

The night was silent, and the sun and moon formed a brilliant tapestry against the black canvas of the sky.

Herodota had fallen asleep, but Geon, unable to for days, remained awake and alert.

He noticed, first, the waters of Hidden Pond beginning to ripple.

Then the earth began to shake, at first a slight tremor and then a violent quake.

Herodota gasped as she awoke. "What is this?" she cried. "What is this, coming into the world…"

RAMP TO HIGH CITY, THÉNAI

It was night, and Khloë and Phalco stood uncertainly, trapped between a battle in the streets below and Old Believers on the High City above.

The moon had fully arisen, and the stars were twinkling, when the ground began a violent tremble.

Screams echoed below, screams so loud that Khloë could hear them.

She heard the *crack* and collapse of pillars, and the sound of crumbling roofs.

The whole earth seemed caught in this violent shake, and below, in the light of lamps and torches, a fissure tore through City Square, splitting it in two.

Khloë screamed; Phalco had fallen on his face.

"Let's go!" Phalco cried. "Let's go! Make a break for it! The harbor! The harbor! Choros!"

They had lost the city to forces they could not control, forces that had not emerged from without, but from within. Escape was Khloë's best chance, and escape was a risk she had to take. "Forward!" she cried. "Forward!"

She scrambled after Phalco as he ran down, toward the site of the battle, toward the harbor that held the only promise of escape. The earthquake continued and the sound of crashing rooftops lit up the evening, emerging over the cacophony of screams.

The night followed after, and the darkness lurking over Thénai was complete.

HARBOR, THÉNAI

Light had begun to emerge over the horizon when Khloë and Phalco found a ship.

The Siren's Claw was headed to Khazidea, but agreed to stop at Choros for the money Phalco had brought along.

There, they would re-form, they would re-group. A graver enemy than the Kersican League had emerged, one that threatened not just Thénai but the wider world, the wider family of humans and amazon-kind.

Choros and Phalco would lead the fight, though they did not know how, they did not know why.

She and Phalco, hand in hand, would battle the Old Believers, in word and deed. Khloë would remain a Thenoan citizen, not for herself, not for even the League, but for the fate of the world itself.

HIDDEN POND, OUTSIDE ARCTOS, ISTEROI KINGDOM

"Ah! Ah! My lords!" Herodota was weeping in the morning, when Geon stirred from his rest. "I have seen her. I have seen the goddess. I will restore her priesthood. I cannot abandon her!"

On the boughs of the pines, a white bird had perched.

How Geon had changed, how utterly he had re-formed, after drinking the holy water, after consuming the spirit in the Stygian Lake.

He had succeeded, though not of his own hand. Rebuilding the priesthood would be a difficult, perhaps impossible task. But he would fight for Amara, and for all the holy gods. He would cleanse the temple, or he would perish in the attempt.

KERSICAN LEAGUE

Weeks Later…

Exhausted and famished, fed only waybread and water for who knew how long, Taicho crossed the border into enemy territory.

The city of slavery, of conquest and of inhumanity, still lay many days away. Kersepoli was where Taicho would find his freedom or perish.

"Look!" Pythio, traveling with them, pointed.

A man on a black horse was galloping toward them. He was dressed for battle, in a breastplate and a red-crested helm.

"Axander! Where have you been?" the Kersican soldier cried. "We have lost so much without you…"

Axander said nothing.

"Have you heard? Have you heard?" the soldier bellowed. "Mount Kronos has erupted again, more furious than ever! Ash and fire and smoke for miles around! It is a baleful sign, if I ever have heard one."

But Taicho had no time for omens, no time for mystic rites or symbolism. He put his hand to his heart. He swore, if he ever escaped, he would return to Thénai. He would make amends for his cowardice. He would save the League, or he would die in the field of battle. He swore an oath to his ancestors under his breath, to his father, to his family, to his village, and to the holy gods.

I will fight! I will fight! I will fight!

EPILOGUE

The battle outside the Temple of Kronos, on the streets below, had quieted.

Elena Kaiaphon had gathered her underlings.

They had moved the statue of the god Kronos back to its place, where it belonged, in the outer sanctuary. The doors were open, baring the god for all to see.

As her underlings chanted, Elena Kaiaphon kissed the statue, its heads and its arms and its chest.

It was so lifelike, so brilliantly forged, and underneath her fingertips, it almost seemed to move.

CONTINUED IN BOOK 9, 'BLADE OF PROPHECY'….

GLOSSARY

CURRENCY

Thalos: A small silver coin, worth one-fourth a doukos. Plural thalon.

Doukos: The standard silver coin across Eloesus. It takes many forms but generally has the city's patron god cast onto the front and the victory laurel wreath on the back. Plural doukon. One doukos is about the daily wage of a skilled laborer.

Oros: A gold coin, worth fifty doukon. Plural orhon.

Talent: A unit of measurement, worth one-thousand doukon.

TERMS

Alabastros: The king of the gods in the Eloesian pantheon. He is revered especially by the Thartans. As king of the gods, he is considered to preside over kingship, leadership, and royalty. He is often depicted as a wise old man. His favored animal is the lion.

Anakhil: In the land of Khazidea, the elite fighting force directly answerable to the king.

Athra: The god of fire in the Southern World. He is also the king of the southron pantheon and is often identified as Alabastros in Eloesian parlance.

Amara: The goddess of motherly love in the Eloesian pantheon. In Thénai and the Amazonian Isles, she is also the goddess of wisdom and battle. Although a mother, she is a virgin. Eloesian legend states she is the daughter of Alabastros and the Earth. Her brother is Tyros, god of war.

Amazonia: A term for amazon lands. Amazonia encompasses the islands of Jogheira, Straiteira, Agathë, Kalormenë and a few smaller islands.

Amazons, the: A race of people living in the coastal islands off the Eloesian shore. Their women are far stronger and—some argue—more intelligent than their men. Though they look similar to humans, amazons and humans cannot breed. The child of an amazon and a human is always stillborn.

Barbarian: A non-Eloesian. The Isteroi and the people of the Ten Cities are often considered barbarians.

Bregantion: A distant colony, located far northwest of Thénai at the mouth of a great river. It is a member of the Thenoan League.

Brekko: The god of wine, song, and theater. He is also considered the King of the Satyrs. He is pictured as a fat man with goat legs, accompanied at all times by his pet panther. According to Eloesian legend, he is the son of Tyros, god of war, and Seladora, goddess of nature. His sister is Nix (see below) whom he fears.

Chiton: A knee-length sleeveless shirt, once popular across Eloesus but now restricted to priests and government officials.

Choros: An island eleven miles northwest of Thénai. As the home for the treasury of the Thenoan League, it is heavily fortified and garrisoned with thousands of troops.

Civic gods: The gods considered sacred to a particular city. Tharta favors Alabastros; Korthos, Nix and Arephon; Kersepoli, Tyros lord of war; and Thénai, Amara.

Demiarch: In the cities of Korthos and Thénai, members of the Assembly.

Dys: A vast peninsula, all the way across the sea, west from Eloesus. Its southwestern edge boasts a number of Eloesian colonies which were originally founded by the city of Tharta. In recent times, the colonies of Dys pledges allegiance to the Thenoan

League due to its promotion of democracy and liberty as opposed to the Kersicans' aristocracy and despotism.

Elehoi: A large underclass, forming the majority of the population of Kersica. They are slaves, captives from Kersepoli's numerous wars, and all Eloesian by birth. The name means "little Eloesian" or "Eloesian-like."

Floridion: A colony, considered impossibly far away, settled by Thenoans in ancient days. It is a member of the Thenoan League.

Free and Democratic Army of Thénai, the: The name of Thénai's army, composed mostly of everyday citizens. As part of schooling, every man is taught to lift a shield and march in formation. The army is led by a Stratego, or general.

High city: A common feature of all Eloesian cities, a towering high ground—natural or man made—which serves as a fortress in times of trouble.

Hoplite: The traditional soldier in the Eloesian army. Each hoplite has a helmet and a breastplate, a spear and a shortsword, in addition to an iron-rimmed wooden shield. When fighting, he locks shields with his fellow hoplites, forming an impenetrable wall as long as he holds formation.

Isteros: A region in the north of Eloesus, along the river Ister. The Isteroi speak a dialect of Eloesian but are thought to be outsiders, due to their pallid complexions and frequently red hair. Arctos, the capital, is much smaller in size than other Eloesian cities.

Kersepoli: A large city, one of the four greatest in Eloesus. It is the most militaristic of the Eloesian cities and is ruled by two kings, either of whom may overrule the other.

Kersica: The region belonging to the city of Kersepoli.

Nymphaeum: A feature in many homes of the rich, a pool made to look like a sacred grotto. In some homes, it is also a place of religious worship and a shrine to Seladora, the goddess of nymphs.

Nix: The goddess of secrets and whispers, her followers call her the Gray Lady or the Queen of Sorcery. She presides over the knowledge of herbs—healing and poisonous—as well as hidden knowledge, wisdom, and the metals iron and silver. She is feared throughout Eloesus, though her name is invoked for protection from the unquiet dead. Korthos was historically the center of her worship. Her favored animals are the owl and the dog. According to Eloesian legend, she is the daughter of Tyros, god of war, and Seladora, goddess of nature. She was hated by her parents and cast out of the household.

Phillipidēs: An Eloesian legendary hero, the son of a Thartan noble who fought in the Megarine War. According to myth, he was given a magic helmet by the goddess Amara which made him invincible to mortal weapons.

Politarch: In the cities of Eloesus, these are the government officials answerable directly to the Assembly. They are charged with certain categories of oversight; thus one politarch might manage the food supply, the other the water. In Korthos and Thénai, they are appointed by the Assembly; in Kersepoli and Tharta they are appointed by kings. Their duties vary from one city to the other.

Slavery: The institution is widespread in Fharas and offers slaves no rights whatsoever; they are viewed as objects or tools, not human beings. In Eloesus, the institution is banned altogether in Thénai and heavily regulated in Korthica and Thartica. Slaves have no rights in Kersepoli.

Southrons: A term for the Fharese, Khazideans, and more generally people from the far south.

Sarxia: A mountainous region in the east of Khazidea. The Thenoan colony of Sarxopoli was founded there in time immemorial, and pledged its allegiance to the league, offering the wealth and materials of its mines.

Stygian waters: Water from a lake in Thenoa (see above), which has long since dried up. The region was, in ancient days, called Stygia after the former city-state of Stygidos. A heavenly being was said to have died in the lake, imbuing the waters with its blood.

Tharta: A great city, considered the chief in Eloesus. It is ruled by a king but has certain limited forms of democracy.

Thénai: A large city, one of the four greatest in Eloesus. It is ruled by an Assembly, elected by the people, and an archon, elected by the Assembly.

Thenoan League: A union of Eloesian city-states with members across the Middle Sea. The headquarters of the League is in Thénai, where the League treasury is located and all League decisions are made.

Thenoa: The lands belonging to Thénai.

Tyros: The god of war. He is revered in Kersepoli; yet he is viewed as never favoring one city over the other, delighting only in battle itself and spilled blood. According to Eloesian legend, he was the son of Alabastros and the Earth. His sister is Amara and his daughter is Nix, whom he hates. His lover is Seladora, goddess of nature.

ABOUT THE AUTHOR

Cursed at birth with a wild imagination, Andrew Cooper spent his youth dreaming of worlds more exciting than Earth.

He is a graduate of the Odyssey Writing Workshop. His stories have appeared in Morpheus Tales, Fear and Trembling, Residential Aliens and Mindflights, among others.

CONTACT THE AUTHOR

Visit **www.aj-cooper.com** to sign up for the newsletter and stay up-to-date on new releases.

Find him on Facebook at:

www.facebook.com/AJCooperauthor